WHEN KARMA COMES TO COLLECT

A. GAVIN

When Karma Comes to Collect

Copyright 2019 by A. Gavin

Published by Mz. Lady P Presents

Life hasn't always been easy for Karma White. At an early age, she knew exactly what it meant to be alone in this cruel world. With a mother that resented her and a father that abandoned her, Karma was left to do everything for herself. Her hopes and dreams were alive, and her future was bright. The only thing missing was true love. That is until Chicago's most eligible bachelor makes his move on her heart.

Lorenzo Lamont is a well-known businessman in the city of Chicago that everyone loves and respects. When he stumbles upon the quirky but gorgeous Karma White, he wants nothing more than to love and cherish her until death does them part. He soon finds out that death is closer than he thought, due to an issue that he chose to ignore that comes back to haunt him. Things take a dramatic turn when Karma finds herself at the receiving end of his anger, fighting for her life.

Will Karma come out on top and take back everything that the darkness stole, or will she succumb to the injuries?

"KAY, why do you have on those big ass glasses and we're inside?"

My best friend reached over the table to try to pull the oversized glasses off my face, but I slapped her hand away. We were sitting in our favorite restaurant downtown trying to enjoy some food and drinks while basking in the summer afternoon breeze. Oya and I made it a habit to always check on each other and spend time together. She was the big sister I never had.

"Oya, I promise you it's nothing. I'm good."

She reached over the table and grabbed the glasses quickly. I held my head down in shame as soon as she gasped. I had run out of my foundation, so I couldn't cover up the handprint turning purple on my honey-colored face. It was never like me to run out of my makeup, but here I was exposed to the world.

"Oh, hell no. Is Zo hitting you again? Karma, you can't keep letting that man pound on you. You're not a punching bag! He's not going to stop until he kills you. Let me help you get away from him, Karma. Please, let me help you."

Oya has known about the abuse for the past few months and has begged me to leave Zo alone. Lorenzo and I had been together for the last three years, and I had been his stress reliever since our six-month anniversary.

What is one to do when the love of their life doesn't turn out to be who you thought they were? My name is Karma White, and I'm in love with a monster.

Lorenzo and I met one day while I was waiting in line to at the local movie theater. I'm a loner and kept to myself most of the time. If I wasn't with Oya, then I was by myself. I ended up spacing out and thought about that day.

Three Years Ago

"One ticket to see the 1:45 p.m. showing of Straight Outta Compton, please." I handed the teller my debit card, but a hand reached out in front of me with a $100 bill.

"Make it two, thanks." I turned around and saw the most gorgeous man that I could have ever laid eyes on.

"Oh no, you didn't have to do that." I held my head down while pushing up my huge prescription glasses. All of a sudden, I felt a hand on my chin, and it lifted my head up.

"Hold your head up, pretty girl. I know I didn't have to, but I wanted to. Would you like to accompany me to this movie?" A smile spread across his face and showed off a perfect set of pearly white teeth. "By the way, I'm Lorenzo. What's your name, ma?"

"My name is Karma, and yes, I'll accompany you to this movie."

Grabbing a strand of my hair, I looked away from Lorenzo and blushed. He placed his hand out for me to take, and I gladly accepted it. I knew I shouldn't have been this accepting of him, but he seemed like such a nice man. Oya was always telling me to live a little, so now I was going to finally take her advice. We ended up stopping by the concession stand to get a few items to enjoy during the movie. Once we were in the theater, we settled in and enjoyed the film. The movie was great per usual, and we exited the theater in pure bliss. I was having so much fun and didn't want the day to end.

"Are you hungry?" he asked as we stepped out into the fresh air. My stomach ended up speaking for me. "That sounds like a yes. Come on. Let's get you fed."

Taking my hand, he led me to his car. After a twenty-minute drive, we ended up at an old-school diner on the south side.

"Welcome to Top Notch. My name is Amanda, and I'll be your server. Can I get you all started on something to drink?" I looked over the menu and decided that I absolutely had to try their strawberry milkshake.

"Can I please have a strawberry milkshake, and can you add crushed Oreos?" She smiled and nodded her head.

"And sir what can I get for you?"

"I'll have what she's having, thank you." She walked off and proceeded to make the milkshakes.

"So, tell me about yourself, Lorenzo." I held my head down as I looked at the menu.

Everything on the menu looked good, but the bacon burger was calling my name. The waitress came back, placed the milkshakes on the table, and took our order. I guess Lorenzo was being a copycat because he ordered the same thing as me.

"Well, I'm Lorenzo Lemont, and I'm twenty-eight years young. I was born and raised on the west side of Chicago, and I'm a business owner. I graduated from the University of Wisconsin Madison with a degree in finance, and I own a few car dealerships throughout the area."

While he was telling me about himself, Amanda came back and placed our food on the table. In no time, we were both digging into our food. I guess I wasn't the only one hungry.

Dipping a fry into my milkshake, I shook my head up and down. Wow, a single man with his head on straight is rare in Chicago. It's safe to say that I am impressed.

"What about you Ms. Karma? Tell me a little about yourself."

"Well I'm Karma White, I'm twenty-three years old, and I graduated from Colombia College here in Chicago. I earned my degree in

English, and I plan to start my own editing company. I'm currently employed as a senior editor, but I want my own business, ya know?"

"You just said a mouthful, pretty girl. What about your childhood? What was that like?" He laughed and shook his head.

"What made you want to buy my ticket and see a movie with me? You don't know me from a can of paint."

I needed to divert his attention to something else. My childhood was a sensitive subject for me. I took a big bite out of my burger and ketchup slid down the side of my face. Lorenzo reached over and wiped my face with a napkin.

"Slow down ma, before you choke on that food. I'm gonna ignore the fact that you deflected from answering my question. But, I saw your gorgeous self walking into the theater and knew that I had to have you. I don't hold back when I want something." He caressed my face with his thumb, and I closed my eyes while letting go of the breath I was holding.

For the rest of our meal, we enjoyed each other's company and got to know one another a little better. Lorenzo paid for our meal and drove me back to my car that I'd left in the theater's parking lot.

"Thank you for today, Lorenzo. It was pretty fun hanging out with you. I don't typically run off with men I just met, but there's something about you that I can't resist. Maybe we can do it again sometime."

I reached for my door, but he pushed it shut and stood in front of me with my back up against the car. He was so close that I could feel his heart beating against my chest.

"Karma, when can I see you again?" Again, I held my head down and blushed.

"When would you like to see me again, Lorenzo?" He placed his hand on his perfectly chiseled face and played in his beard.

"Can I see you tonight?"

Flicking my wrist, my Apple watch turned on and showed that it was only about to be six p.m.

"How does ten o'clock sound?" Never in my life had I been so *forward with a man, but with Lorenzo, I felt myself breaking out of my introvert shell.*

"Then I'll see you at ten o'clock, beautiful. Here, lock your number and address in my phone. I'll call when I'm on my way." Doing as he instructed I placed my number and address into his phone. He leaned in and placed a soft kiss on my cheek. "I'll see you in a few, pretty girl."

Opening my car door, I climbed in and laid my head on the headrest.

555-7899: *Drive safely, pretty girl.*

Me: *Thanks, you too, Lorenzo. See you soon.*

555-7899: *Please call me Zo.*

I needed to call Oya and tell her what was going on. Knowing her, she wouldn't believe me. Pressing her name on the screen, I dialed her up. After three rings she answered.

"What's up, ma? Everything good? How was the movie?" She sounded like she was at the salon. Oya was a hair stylist and had her own shop located in the South Loop. She was well known all over the city.

"The movie was great, but something else happened." I proceeded to tell her everything that happened with Lorenzo and me. When I was done, there wasn't a sound from the other end of the phone. "Hello? Oya, are you there?"

"Ahhhhhh!!!" she screamed, and I had to turn the volume down on my car speakers.

"Oya, oh my god, what's wrong? Is everything okay?" I busted a U-turn in the middle of the street and headed straight to Oya's shop. The shop was only fifteen minutes away from the movie theater.

"Yes! Karma is finally about to get some dick! Ayyyeee!!!" This chick did the absolute most. I pulled over to the side of the road in order to slow down my elevated heart rate.

"Bitch, I thought something was wrong with you! Don't scare me like that!" Resting my head against the seat, I closed my eyes and took some deep breaths.

The knocking at my door caused my eyes to pop open, and Lorenzo was staring back at me. I jumped out of my seat, and my Apple watch's heart monitor started beeping informing me that my heart rate was too high. At this point, Oya was in the background screaming at me, and Lorenzo continued to knock on the window.

"I need everyone to calm down!" I yelled. "Oya, give me a few minutes, and I'll be at your shop. I have to deal with something really quick."

I hung up the phone before she could get a word in. Why was Lorenzo at my window? Pressing the window down button, I looked up and saw that he had a scowl on his face.

"What's wrong, Ma? I saw you bust a U-turn in the middle of the street and then pull over. Is everything okay?" The words wouldn't come out of my mouth due to the fact that I was trying to steady my heartbeat. Finally, after a few deep breaths, I was good to go.

"Yes, sorry to give you a scare. My best friend gave me a scare as well, and I was on my way to her until she told me everything was okay. I'm on my way home now. I'll see you at ten." He nodded his head and walked away.

Twenty minutes later, I arrived at my loft in the West Loop. A friend of mine leased out an industrial two-story loft, and I had transformed it into my dream home. Opening my door, I kicked off my shoes and placed them on the welcome mat. I hated wearing shoes inside my home. No one was allowed to wear shoes in my house. I was a slight germaphobe. It was going on 6:30, so I had plenty of time to relax and get ready before Lorenzo arrived. After I was showered and moisturized, I lay in my bed allowing the cool air to run over my body as I drifted off to sleep.

The buzzing of my alarm stirred me out of my sleep. Looking at the clock, I saw that it was now nine p.m. Lorenzo was due here in an hour. Stepping out of bed, I found my way to my bathroom and fresh-

ened up. While brushing my teeth, I planned the perfect outfit in my head. Since we were hanging here at my house, I decided to keep it simple. I grabbed a comfortable off the shoulder sweater and a pair of mesh leggings. Once I was dressed, I slid on a pair of my fuzzy socks and threw my curly hair into a messy high bun. I felt like I was dressed too casually, so I decided to FaceTime Oya.

"What's up—wait a minute. Aren't you having company tonight? I hope you aren't wearing that? You know what? I'm on my way. Give me ten minutes."

"Oya! Wait—" She hung up the phone.

Exactly ten minutes later, Oya was using her key to get into my apartment.

"Ladybug, come in here so that I can turn you into the sex goddess you are! I'm sure he will be on time, so we have less than thirty minutes to make a miracle happen."

Oya had transformed me into a brand new person. I looked in the mirror, and I was in love with the final result. She dressed me in a burgundy mesh cropped top with distressed white jeans. We topped it off with a long white cardigan. It was chill but sexy in the same sense. She kept my hair in the messy bun but laid my edges to perfection. Adding a few small accessories topped the look off.

"Ladybug, you look amazing. Now sit so that I can give your face a light beat." Sitting down at my vanity, Oya applied the makeup to my face effortlessly. "Done, now let me get out of here before he sees me. Have fun Ladybug and don't over think this. Just call me if he turns out to be crazy. I'm only a few floors away." She kissed me on my cheek, gathered her belongings, and rushed out of the door. It paid to have your best friend living only a few floors above you.

For my final touch, I sprayed on my favorite fragrance from Bath & Body Works, Pearberry. Looking down at my phone, I saw that Lorenzo had texted.

Lorenzo: *Hey beautiful, I'm on my way. I'm going to stop by and get some food. Is there anything in particular that you'd like?*

Me: *Whatever you choose, I'll be more than happy with. Be safe. See you soon.*

I was a ball of nerves right now, so I decided to grab a glass of wine. After a few sips, I was finally cool, calm, and collected.

My doorbell rang, and I dashed to the intercom system buzzing Lorenzo up. Before he made it in, I decided to give myself a little pep talk. This was the first time in a long time that I had a man genuinely interested in me. Most guys viewed me as a nerdy girl with no sense of adventure, and that was far from the truth. I loved hanging out and doing things, but I also liked sitting at home with a glass of wine and reading a good book. It's all about balance.

As I was pacing the floor, there was a light knock on the door. Taking a deep breath, I opened the door and looked at the handsome man standing in front of me. In one hand, he held a bottle of wine and a bag of food, and in the other, he held a beautiful bouquet of flowers. He had on a simple white t-shirt and a pair of dark blue Levi jeans. I moved to the side to let him in and grabbed the flowers and wine from him. I turned around to ask him to take his shoes off, but he had beat me to the punch.

"Nice place you have here," he said, walking up to me and placing a kiss on my cheek. My knees started to get a little weak once I got a whiff of his cologne.

"Th-thank you." I smiled nervously and placed the items on my kitchen island.

"Relax ma, I got you, okay?" He grabbed my hand and led me to the couch. "Have a seat. Let me make the plates." Words had escaped me, but I was able to nod my head.

For the remainder of the evening, we ate, drank, and joked around while watching TV. I found myself falling asleep on his shoulder during a movie that I had no interest in. The next thing I knew I was being lifted off of the couch and carried to my room.

"Come on, let's get you into bed. I'm gonna get outta here," he said *as he placed soft kisses on my forehead. I'm not sure what came over me, but the next words out of my mouth shocked me.*

"Stay with me." I held my head down in fear that he was going to say no. That is until he lifted my chin and placed a soft yet passionate kiss on my lips.

"I'd love to stay with you."

From that night on we were inseparable.

Present Day

"Karma, are you listening to me?" Oya, snapped her fingers in my face as I came back to reality. A single tear slid down my face as I reminisced on a simpler but happy time in our relationship. Quickly taking my napkin, I wiped the tear away.

"Yes, sorry I'm listening. I know it's still early, but please don't be mad at me. I'm supposed to be home by five p.m. I hate to leave you, but I gotta get going." Oya looked at me with disappointment written all over her face.

"I'm begging you, Ladybug. Please don't go back there. Let me help you." Tears started streaming down her beautiful chocolate covered skin, and my heart broke into a million pieces. It pained me to see my best friend in such a distraught state of mind, and it was all my fault.

"Oya, I'll be fine. He's just going through a rough patch. It'll be over with soon. I promise. Now, I'm already late. I have to go." Not wanting to hear anymore, I placed a few bills on the table, kissed her cheek, and ran to my awaiting Uber.

As the Uber pulled up to our home, my stomach started to turn. Something was going to happen tonight, but I didn't know what. I thanked the driver and made my way to our beautiful wooden double doors. Looking down at my watch, I noticed that it was ten minutes past my curfew. Yes, at the age of twenty-six, I had a curfew and not a reasonable one. Unfortunately, the deep breaths I just took did not prepare me for what I was about to endure. After twisting the knob and stepping past the threshold, I was met with a blur.

"Ahhh!" I fell onto the cold marble floor while holding my face and stomach. "Zo, stop! I'm sorry! There was traffic. You can look at my Uber log to see I'm telling you the truth. Please just stop hitting me."

My body curled into the fetal position as I cried out in pain. Lorenzo had delivered two smacks to my face and one punch to my stomach. The impact from the punch caused me to vomit on the floor. He delivered three punches to my jaw, and it was broken on the first impact.

"You's a nasty ass bitch!" He grabbed me by my hair and shoved my face into the pile of vomit. "Eat that shit since you went out and spent my hard earned money on it. That's all you do! Shop, eat, and spend my money! You're a worthless piece of shit, Karma."

At this point it caused me to vomit even more. My stomach was weak, and I threw up at the sight of anyone regurgitating.

"Lorenzo, stop, please. I'm sorry!" It pained me to talk, but I needed the beating to stop.

My cries fell on deaf ears. He wrapped my long hair around his massive hands and drugged me up the marble staircase. My long but small frame bounced on each step as we made our way to where ever Zo was leading me. I kicked and screamed for dear life because I could feel my hair detaching from my scalp. We lived in a very secluded area so no one could hear me. I was used to a few hits here and there, and maybe a slam against the wall, but today, was different. Today's beating was a whole new level. I knew that me being late for curfew couldn't have caused this rage. Something was deeply wrong with Zo.

"Zo, you're hurting me. Baby, I'll do whatever it takes. Please just stop. I'll do whatever it takes."

We made it to the master bathroom, and he threw me against the sink. He then proceeded to turn on the bath water. I'm not sure why I did this, but I tried crawling away from him, as quickly as my battered body would allow.

"You tryna leave me? Oh no, I don't think so. We're in this for life!" He yanked me up by my shirt and tore it open exposing the upper half of my body. "So you're out here like you don't have a man at home, Karma? Where's your bra? Who are you trying to impress? You know what, I'm sick of this shit."

He banged my head on the side of the tub, and I heard my nose crack. Blood poured down my face like a leaky faucet. A lump had now formed in my throat, and I was unable to scream anymore. My body was exhausted. I was tired of fighting. Lorenzo was just too strong. Defeat had set in. He won.

In one swift motion, Zo picked me up and threw me in the tub. Again, he wrapped my hair around his knuckles and dunked my head under the scolding hot water. As I tried to scream and fight, water filled my lungs, and I began to choke. He pulled me back up and punched me in my right eye. He continued this abuse until my eyes were swollen and I was gasping for air. Releasing my hair, he ran away and left me in the tub clinging on for life.

As I was searching for a breath, I noticed that my Apple Watch was still on my wrist. I pressed the button with what little strength I had and asked Siri to call Oya. The pain in my mouth was unbearable, but I needed to do this in order to save my life.

"Hello? Karma, are you there? Speak to me, Karma!" I continued to struggle with catching my breath. I felt like I was drowning above water. "Oh god, what did he do? I'm calling the police. Stay with me. Please stay with me. I should never have let you leave!!"

"Help..." was all I would get out before my body shut down, and I slid into the tub, and I drew my last breath.

CHAPTER TWO
KARMA WHITE

"COME ON, people! We're losing her! Ms. White, can you hear me? Ma'am, if you can hear me squeeze my hand. Oh god, she's coding. Start the chest compressions. Ms. White, we're going to do everything we can to save you. Stay with me. Please stay with me. Come on, sweetie. Please stay with me."

What did I do to deserve this? Did I not love him enough? Was the food cold when he got home? These were just some of the questions running through my head as I lay here on this stretcher fighting for my life. One would think that I would be saying my peace with the Lord and asking him to forgive me of my sins, but here I am, asking what I did wrong to Lorenzo instead of worry about whether I'll live to see another day.

"Stats are starting to improve. Let's give her something for the pain and come back to check on her in a little while. Hopefully, she'll come back to us soon. She's lucky to have a friend like you."

When I tried to open my eyes, only a sliver of light shined through. I tried to move my head from side to side, but the pain was unbearable. When I went to scream for help, my mouth wouldn't open. All I could do was sob silently and hope that someone would come to me soon.

"Oh my gosh. Ladybug, I'm right here. Thank you, Lord!" I heard Oya's voice, but I couldn't see her. It caused me to cry even harder. "Shhh, don't cry, everything will be okay... Nurse! Somebody, please! She's awake."

"Well if it isn't the strongest woman in the world. Karma, welcome back. You gave us quite a scare."

I used what little strength I had and pointed to my mouth so that they could understand that I wanted to talk.

"I'm sorry honey. Let me get the doctor in here to explain everything. By the way, I'm Ms. Rose, and I'll be taking care of you during the evening shifts. Karen will be here in the mornings, but you won't like her nearly as much as you'll like me." I heard Oya snicker as she ran her fingers through my hair.

"Hello Ms. White, glad to have you back with us. You gave us quite the scare. I'm Dr. Bismale, and I wanted to come in and explain some things to you. I'm going to hold your hand and if this is too much to bear just give my hand a light squeeze and I'll stop talking and give you a minute to collect yourself. First things first we are thankful that you are here with us. If you didn't take the time to call your friend, things could have been much worse. At this time I'm going to run down a list of your injuries.

Like I said if this is too much, just squeeze my hand. Your eyes are swollen shut, but no damage was done to them. The swelling will decrease in a few days. Just give that time. Two of your ribs on your right side are cracked, but those will heal on their own with rest, ice, and pain medication. Your nose was broken, but it will heal with time as well. Now on to the most important yet grueling injury. You have a fractured jaw that required us to wire it shut in order for it to heal. The healing times varies, but it can be anywhere between six to eight weeks. You'll be on a liquid diet for some time, but we will get you back and better than ever. Now I would like to keep you for a few days for observation, and then we'll work on getting you released. Rest up and page Ms. Rose if you start to feel any discomfort. She'll come and administer the pain medication."

With that, the doctor walked out and closed the door. That's when the waterworks started. What had my life become? How did I allow myself to get to this point?

"Oh, Ladybug, please don't cry." I felt her wiping the tears off my face, but I couldn't collect myself. Things had gone too far. Who would do that to someone they claim to love? "Ladybug, I have to go, but Ms. Rose is here, and she's been taking excellent care of you. She knows to call me if you need me. We have a routine down pat. Get some rest." I heard her press a button, and a wave of cold liquid flowed through my body.

Sometime later I woke up from the sounds of my machines beeping and a hand caressing my hair. Panic began to set in when a familiar scent invaded my nostrils. My heart monitor began beeping rapidly, but after a few seconds, the beeping disappeared. My finger heart monitor had been removed. Then the voice that I was dreading to hear filled the room.

"Karma," he took a deep breath and stayed silent for a minute. "I don't know why I keep doing this. Shit is rough out here, but I promise things are going to get better. I'm so sorry for what I did. I swear that I love you with everything in me, and I-I'm gonna get the help I need. Please just let me take you home and let some people come and take care of you. Private doctors and around the clock nurses will be there to help in your recovery."

If I didn't know him, I would have believed him. But I did, and I knew that it wasn't sincere. I tried feeling for the remote to call the nurse, but the room was pitch black. I could feel his cold lips on my forehead, and I tried to move as best as I could to shake him off of me. His touch caused my body to shutter from pure and utter disgust.

"W-why are you acting like this. I didn't mean to do it, Karma. It's just that you make me so mad sometimes. You should know what I do and don't like by now. You have gotta stop doing the things you do to piss me off."

He placed more kisses on my forehead, and I felt something wet on my face. Was he crying? This was new to me. Not once had he ever cried after one of our run-ins. My suspicions were confirmed when I heard a sniffle, but I knew better. He was putting on a show to try to get me to come back home with him.

"Pretty girl, will you come back home?" When I didn't respond to his question, his mood instantly changed. It's as if he didn't know that I couldn't respond. My mouth was wired shut.

Dumb ass.

"Karma, now I asked nicely. There are only two ways you're getting out of here. It's either with me, or it's in a body bag. Take your pick."

My soul was crying out to God asking him why me? Why did this man have to come into my life? I shook my head as best as I could and started sobbing uncontrollably. The movements and sobbing hurt more than anything I had ever experienced in life, and the pain caused me to cry even harder.

"Shut up!" he said through gritted teeth. "This is why I do what I do!"

My pillow was pulled from under me causing my head to bounce against the mattress. As I was focusing on that pain, I felt the fabric of the pillow on my face, and I could no longer breathe.

"See you in hell," was all I heard.

With all of his strength, he held the pillow until my body began to shake uncontrollably. I just knew I was about to die, so I said a prayer and asked God to let me die quickly and for him to take care of Oya.

"What is going on in here? Who are you—"

I heard a loud crash, and Ms. Rose screamed out. She yelled out a few other obscenities as I focused on getting air into my lungs.

"The police and doctor are on their way, sweetie. I'm gonna put this oxygen mask on you. Take slow and deep breaths. Oh father

God, watch over her," she continued to pray over me until the doctor and officers approached.

"He's a coward! Y'all better find him befo' I do!" she yelled out.

The doctor performed a few tests and spoke with the police. They spoke with Ms. Rose for a few minutes and came to the conclusion that they were going to move me to a private room with twenty-four-hour monitoring. Ms. Rose exhaled and cried out to the heavens. They asked Ms. Rose if she got a good look at the offender, but she said she didn't. I couldn't help in my condition, but when I'm able to, I will damn sure try.

"I'm going to give Oya a call to let her know what's going on. Baby, you sit back and rest. You won't feel a thing in a minute." That familiar and wonderful cold liquid shot through my body, and I was out like a light and off to dreamland.

Six Months Into The Relationship

Staring in the floor length mirror in front of me I admired every inch of my being. The long gold, sequence, spaghetti strapped dress fit my body like a glove, but that wasn't the best part it. The low cut in the back was the star of the show, along with the thigh-high slip that elongated my already long legs. My long hair was in a high bun at the top of my head, and I must say that I was feeling like a million bucks. My girl Rhyland Pierre had finally opened her beauty bar, and she had me looking like my best self. Tonight was a special night, and I needed to look the part.

"You look gorgeous." Zo came behind me, wrapped his arms around my waist, and placed a soft kiss on my neck.

"Well, you don't look too bad yourself, Mr. Lamont. Let me fix this bowtie for you." I straightened out his bowtie and admired the man standing in front of him. Today was our six-month anniversary. Whenever I was with him, it was as if I was floating on a cloud. I couldn't help but smile on the inside and out whenever I heard his voice or smelled that Jean Paul Gaultier cologne.

"What's got you smiling, pretty girl?" He placed a few more kisses on my collarbone, and I had to stop him, or we wouldn't be making it to this event.

"Baby, if you don't stop we aren't going to be on time. You don't want to be late for this evening now do you?" He grinned at me and licked his lips. "No Mr. Lamont, you will not." I started to back away from him, and he pulled back and attacked me with his lips.

"I'm the boss, and I can do what I want to do. And if I want to make love to the woman of my dreams before a boring charity dinner, then that's exactly what I'm going to do."

In one swift motion, he picked me up and placed me over his shoulder. He reached his hand under my dress, moved my thong to the side, and began rotating his thumb around my throbbing pearl. Throwing me on the bed, he began removing his tie, but his phone ringing stopped him. He took a deep breath and rolled his eyes while looking down at the bulge in his pants. I couldn't help but giggle. It was clear that he was frustrated because sex wasn't going to happen right now.

When I rolled over to get out of the bed, he snarled at me. I blew him a kiss and went to our master bathroom to freshen up. I refused to attend this event smelling like my own natural juices.

After taking care of my hygiene, I decided to check on Zo. He was seated on the bed on the bed flipping through his phone. Leaning against the doorframe, I admired the man in front of me. Everything about him screamed boss, and I loved every inch of him.

"Baby, let's go before we're late." He looked at me with love in his eyes, and I knew that he was the man that I was going to marry.

Tonight, was a big night for Lorenzo, people from all over the country were gathered here for his annual charity event. He was passionate about his business, but he cared more about giving back to the community that raised him. Politicians, music executives, and so

many other people were in attendance. Arriving at the venue, I decided to check myself out in the visor one last time. Zo gave me a nod of approval, and we stepped out of the car like royalty. He held his arm out for me, and I happily wrapped mine in his. I was honored to be the lady on his arm. Even though this isn't how I pictured us spending our anniversary, I smiled brightly because as long as I'm with him, I didn't care.

The night was young as music filled the room while the people enjoyed good food and drinks. Like a good woman, I was working the room with ease. Lorenzo was admired and loved by so many. I was currently speaking with a few gentlemen that were interested in investing money into Zo's children center. This was a big deal, and I couldn't be happier for him.

"Ms. Karma, Lorenzo is a very lucky man to have you on his team. You speak with such elegance and poise." He wrapped his arm around my waist and gave me a side hug. If I didn't know any better, I would have thought nothing of the gesture, but when his thumb caressed my arm, I knew I needed to step away.

That ended up being the pattern for the evening. I was mixing and mingling with a few of Lorenzo's partners, but they were making me a little uncomfortable. However, I didn't want to draw any unnecessary attention on Zo's big day. I wanted him to come to save me, but he was working the room just like I was.

"Excuse me. Can I have everyone's attention, please? I'd like to thank each and every one of you for coming out and sharing this evening with me. As everyone knows I was born and raised here in Chicago and nothing brings me more joy than giving back to the community. All of the proceeds from this evening will help support kids just like me."

He smiled showing off his perfect teeth, and I got lost in him as he continued to address the crowd.

"Last but not least, I'd like to thank the special lady in my life. Thank you for sticking by me as my team, and I worked tirelessly to plan this event. You're a true rockstar, and I thank you for putting up

with me." He laughed along with the crowd, and I was waiting for him to look my way, but the look never came. I found it odd, but I decided to shake off any negative thoughts that were coming my way.

An hour had passed after Zo gave his speech, and I had yet to spend any time with him, so I decided to excuse myself out of a conversation and go look for the man of the night. He was posted on the opposite side of the room talking to a beautiful younger woman and a handsome man. I couldn't help it, but I found myself studying him. His chocolate complexion looked soft and smooth like butter. His eyes were almond shaped and low, but the thing that caught my attention was his mannerisms. His presence commanded attention and he most definitely had mine. Our eyes connected, and I had to look away immediately. Thankfully, Zo hadn't noticed anything.

As I continued to stand off to the side, I noticed that the young lady was hanging onto Lorenzo's every word. He must have been telling one hell of a joke because she was dying of laughter along with caressing his arm. The little touches here and there were causing a jealous rage to flow through me. The gentleman that was with them excused himself, and Lorenzo and the young lady continued to talk. He whispered in her ear and had this milk chocolate cutie blushing like a schoolgirl. I didn't even think girls her complexion could blush.

Our eyes connected, and I quickly looked away. Out the corner of my eye, I could see that she was telling him something. She placed a kiss on his cheek and walked away. My heart was telling me that this was innocent, but my mind was screaming to beat her ass. Lorenzo had never given me a reason to believe that he was cheating on me, so I calmed myself down and decided that it was completely innocent. I continued to study his moves as he walked over to the bar. He downed two shots of brown liquid and then made his way over to me.

The energy that was moving towards me scared me. Something was wrong with him, and I needed to figure it out. The smell of whiskey slapped me in the face before he approached me. He was going to be good and drunk.

"Baby, is everything okay?" His eyes trained on me, and they were now bloodshot red.

"Go wait in the car for me. We're leaving." The night wasn't even halfway done.

"But this is your—"

He walked up to me and pulled me close to him by my waist. The alcohol was thick on his breath as he spoke through gritted teeth. He dug his fingernails into my side, and the pain was becoming unbearable.

"You're so fuckin' hardheaded. Just do what the fuck I said."

I was in absolute shock. Not once had he ever spoken to me like this. I quickly grabbed my clutch and ran to the car trying to avoid anyone seeing the tears streaming down my face.

Thankfully, the car was directly in front of the venue, so I climbed in and put my head in my hands. Lorenzo got in about ten minutes after me and drove us home. No words were said during the thirty-minute drive, and that was fine with me. Eventually, we were going to have to talk about this, but for now, the silence was needed.

We pulled in front of the house, and Lorenzo exited the car without even coming to open my door. He was a few feet in front of me and walked in the door first. As soon as I stepped to the door, it slammed in my face. He had lost his natural born mind. I was more than convinced at this point. I should have walked away and called myself a cab, but I decided to open the door and walk in.

As quickly as I could, I slipped in and decided to go to another room in the house. I wasn't sure where he went, and at this point, I really didn't care to, but I refused to go to his room. If his attitude didn't change soon, then I would just go back to my apartment. I was smart enough to keep it after he asked me to move in two months after knowing him. Oya helped me keep it a secret by placing the lease in her name. The landlord was a friend and was cool with it, as long as the rent was getting paid.

Sitting on the bed, I focused on removing my shoes and trying to figure out what was wrong with Zo. I wouldn't think too hard about it, but I really wanted to know. A million different scenarios ran through my head, but I decided to stop before it got too deep. It was time for me to shake off those thoughts and get into my nightly routine. The shower was going to put my mind at ease.

The mixture of the hot water and the lavender exfoliating scrub that I was using was enough to put my mind at ease, and I could feel myself instantly relaxing.

"Karma, where are you?" he screamed. That lasted all of five minutes, so much for a relaxing shower. I should have followed my first mind and went home.

"I'm in the shower!" I yelled back. I hope it took him a little longer to find me since I wasn't in his master bathroom.

Unfortunately, for me, luck wasn't on my side. The shower door swung open, and the devil himself was staring back at me. His eyes were an even darker shade of red, and his chest heaved up and down like a rabid dog.

"Why aren't you in our room?" His words were slurred, and he reeked of alcohol. He must have come in the house and headed straight to the bar in his man cave.

"Babe, you seem a little agitated, so I decided to give you some space to clear your head and regain control of your emotions."

I thought the conversation would have been over, so I turned my back on him and released my locks out of the bun. The sound of the shower door flying off the hinges and shattering on the floor caused me to turn around just in time for his fist to connect with my face. The impact of the hit sent me flying across the shower making me slip and slide down the wall.

Dreaming about the first time Zo laid his hands on me caused me to jump out of my sleep. I don't know how long I had been sleeping, but something felt different. The struggle to open my eyes wasn't anything new, but this time, when I tried, it was different. Immediately, I started to cry. I was finally able to open my eyes and see again. I'm sure that I looked a hot mess, but at this point, it didn't matter. The fact that my sight wasn't lost due to the abuse was more than enough to make me cry tears of joy. It was a little blurry, but that was normal. I couldn't see before the beating, so that was expected.

The sounds of soft snoring startled me, but when I looked to my left Oya was snuggled in a blanket sleeping peacefully. I wanted to smile at the sight before me, but my wired mouth wouldn't allow it. The fact that she had been here nonstop let me know that I had a true friend in her. I would forever be in debt to her. The encounter that I had with Zo had left me a little on edge.

I had been observing my surroundings for a little while, and then the room door began to open. My heart rate started to increase because I didn't know who was entering the room. I felt defenseless due to my injuries. A feeling of relief came over me when I saw that it was Ms. Rose.

Over the next twenty minutes, the doctors ran tests to make sure that I was healing properly. After the picking and probing, they were finally done. Unfortunately, I wouldn't be leaving this hospital any time soon. It was time for me to get comfortable.

CHAPTER THREE
OYA ZAIRE

SEEING my best friend hurt and abused must be one of the hardest things that I've ever had to endure. However, no matter what, I was going to remain here for her. Karma didn't know it, but her situation hit close to my home. When I was younger, I witnessed my mother lose herself in my father. She gave him everything she had to offer, but it still wasn't enough. I had the chance to save her, but due to fear and adolescence, I failed. Here I was being given a second chance to save someone I care about.

I could feel her eyes burning into me as I was daydreaming. It's been a few days since she was able to fully open her eyes, but her mouth was still wired shut. We were only able to communicate by her writing down what she needed, so I went and purchased her a dry erase board from Target. She started scribbling away, and I just knew she was about to ask me something. When she held up the sign, I had to think about my answer. She asked me what I was thinking about.

"I'm thinking about you, Ladybug. I hate that you're right there, and I couldn't save you."

A single tear slid down my cheek, but I quickly wiped it away.

She held up the sign and told me to stop crying. I quickly wiped the tears away and thought about the last time I cried.

Thirteen Years Ago

Today was a day unlike any other. Throughout the day, I kept having a funny feeling in my stomach that I couldn't shake. It started as soon as I left the house and bothered me through each and every class. I've never felt this before, and I was beginning to worry. I just wanted this school day to end and run home to climb in my bed. Nevertheless, before I knew it, the end of the day bell rang, and I darted out of the building quicker than a bolt of lightning.

Making it through the entryway of my home, I heard the familiar sounds of my mother and father arguing. My parents have been at odds with each other for the last few years. However, my mother never folded and continued to stand by my father and support him no matter what. The yelling was normal, so I made my way to my room and put on my headphones. Drowning them out with my music was the best thing for me.

As I lay in bed, I tried to drown out the noise, but tonight it was louder than I've ever experienced. I hated that my mother stayed and continued to give him her all. Time and time again, I begged her to leave, but she always told me to stay in a child's place.

The loud bang followed by shattering glass caused me to jump out of my bed to see what was going on. The arguing between my parents wasn't unusual, but tonight something was different. When I walked into their room, I was horrified at the sight in front of me. My mother was sitting under her full-length mirror holding the back of her head and screaming at the top of her lungs. Looking over at my father, I noticed that he was foaming by the mouth and yelling, but what scared me the most was the shiny gun in his hands pointed at my mother.

"Daddy, no!" I yelled through the tears.

"Leave now, Oya!" his voice boomed throughout the room, and it

caused me to jump. *"This was bound to happen. She's wicked and no good for me."*

Never in my life have I heard my father speak about my mother this way. I had no clue what he meant. My only focus was to save the woman who did any and everything she could for this family.

I went over to her and held her while crying and screaming at my father to put the gun down. Examining my mother, I noticed that she was bleeding profusely from her head wound.

"Papa, we need to get her to the hospital! I promise I won't tell them what happened. Please, just let me save her!"

"No one is coming up in this house to save her. Do you understand me? She has wronged me for the last time!"

It was clear that he wasn't going to save her. I was her last hope. Doing the unthinkable, I used every ounce of strength in my body and lunged at him. We tussled back and forth, and I was determined to get the gun out of his hands. The crazed look in his eyes caused me to fight harder. The person staring back at me was someone I had never seen before.

As we fought, I prayed that we all made it out of here alive. In the blink of an eye, he shoved me off him sending me flying across the room and fired the gun.

Karma snapped her fingers bringing me back to reality. I didn't even realize that I had mentally checked out.

"I'm going to be okay. Is there anything I can get you?"

She scribbled what she needed, and I agreed to get it. It gave me a chance to take a breather. Honestly, being in that room was bringing back feelings that I had suppressed a long time ago. Kissing her forehead, I walked out the door and got in my car.

"Call from Mase, press the pick-up button to answer the call!" my Bluetooth speaker shouted.

"Hey babe," I answered.

"Aye, where you at?" Damn, no warm greeting.

"Heading to Target. K needed a few things—" He sighed heavily, and I knew this wasn't going to be a friendly conversation.

"Yo, I get that she's ya friend and everything, but have you taken any time for yaself? Have you eatin' anything today? Between the shop and taking care of her, you ain't did shit for Oya."

Mase has been my boyfriend for the past three years, and things with us were different. He was all about me but didn't take well to my close friendship with Karma. I saw an opportunity to help my friend, and I decided to take it. I once made a mistake of not helping someone sooner, and I refused to do it again.

"Mase, yes, I've eaten, and yes, I'm taking care of myself. I appreciate your concern, but I'm fine."

I tried to stay as cheerful as I could. If Mase hinted that something was wrong, he would be all over me like white on rice. I loved that he cared about me, but it felt like he was smothering me.

"Oya, don't make me bring my ass to that hospital and show the fuck out."

We spoke a little longer, and then I went and got the things Karma needed. Hopefully, we wouldn't be in the hospital too much longer. I quickly grabbed the things she needed and went back to the hospital.

It's been about two weeks, and Karma was improving. The doctors were hopeful that she would be released within the next few days. That was the best news that I'd heard all day. She was starting to get a little stir crazy, and I couldn't lie, I was too.

"You ready to go home, Ladybug?" She nodded and smiled a little, but the smile faded as quickly as it had come. In that instant, I knew that I had asked the wrong question.

"Don't worry, you're safe, and I got you. I'm not going to let anything happen to you. I put that on my life."

I continued to talk to her for a little bit before Rose came back in for her hourly check-up. Rose absolutely loved Karma just like anyone that had come in contact with her. She even picked up extra shifts to help Karma during her recovery.

"Hey Rose, do you ever take a break?" She put her hands on her hip and started to sass me.

"Don't worry about me, child. I'm running better than women half my age. It's something about this one right here that makes me want to make sure she's good." She continued to do her routine checkup and then took a seat near the bed.

"Sweetheart, do you know what you are going to do after they release you?" Karma took a deep breath and shrugged.

"Well, if you're up to it, I have room at my house. My grandson felt the need to buy me a huge house even though it's just me. I have plenty of room for you. That's if you choose to stay. Plus, I can keep an eye on you and help you recover with your wires." Karma looked at Ms. Rose with tear-filled eyes. I started to tear up too. She needed this in her life.

CHAPTER FOUR
KARMA WHITE

RELEASE DAY

TODAY WAS RELEASE DAY, and I couldn't be happier. Lord knows the team at Christ Hospital was doing an amazing job, and I hated to leave them, but it was time for me to go. Oya agreed to pick me up, and I was grateful for her. We were going to head to the house that I shared with Lorenzo so that I could grab the rest of my things. Thankfully, my phone still connected to Zo's calendar, and it showed that he was out of town. My spirit was happy. I could go the rest of my life not seeing him.

We arrived at the house, and a wave of sadness washed over me. Here I was, back at the scene of the crime. The police had been questioning me and asking me who did it, but I wasn't giving any information. Unfortunately, I was too scared of Lorenzo coming back and finishing what he started.

"You don't have to do this. We don't have to go inside. You still have things at the apartment, and whatever you don't have, we can get. You have a decent amount of money saved to live off of until you're fully healed."

I heard her loud and clear, but I had some things that I needed that I just couldn't be replaced. I hated that I couldn't talk and reassure her that I would be fine. My time in the hospital taught me so much about my own personal strength, and I was determined to show Oya just how far I had come.

The walk to the door was probably one of the hardest things I had done in a while. I placed my key into the lock, and surprisingly it still worked. Maybe he thought that we were going to try again. I really hoped that wasn't the case.

Oya grabbed my hand and led me into the house. Walking into the foyer, flashbacks of that day come to the forefront of my mind. My face began to sting as I thought about the first smack that he had ever delivered to me. Tears started to form in my eyes, but at this point, I was tired of crying. I wiped away the little tear and got right to work. I didn't want to stay here longer than I needed to. Cleaning out my side of the closet was going to take the longest, so that's where I decided to get started.

As I made it to the room that we shared, I could still smell the Jean Paul Gaultier cologne penetrating the air. It used to make me feel warm and fuzzy inside, but now the smell enraged me. I shook the feeling off and pulled clothes off the hanger.

An hour later, my things were in the truck and ready to go.

"Ladybug, you ready to go?" Oya called out from the door. As I stood at the top of the stairs, something came over me.

I looked at her and shook my head. There was something that needed to be done. So, I ran downstairs to Zo's man cave. He was big on sports and kept all sorts of memorabilia. His Louisville Slugger was mounted on the wall signed by his favorite White Sox player Harold Baines. The first time he invited me to his house he explained why he loved his man cave so much. He had memorabilia from all his favorite players. However, the big attraction here was his trophy case.

The trophy case held every single award that he had won during his sports career from elementary school to college. He was so proud of this case, and now that I think about it, it was making me sick to my stomach. The last thing that was placed in here was a picture that he took with Khalil Mack after he was traded to the Chicago Bears from the Oakland Raiders. The smile on his face was enough to make my blood boil and my skin to start smoking. If only people knew the monster behind that smile.

The visions of the beating returned to my head and the pain that I had been feeling for the past month or so had now turned into pure and utter hatred. I hated everything that this man stood for. Truth be told, if I could, I would inflict that same pain on him.

"Mmmm!" I screamed out as best as I could.

This man had hurt me so bad, and there was no going back. I would have to live with these memories for the rest of my life. How was I going to deal with knowing that the man that I gave every ounce of me to betray me?

Without warning, I grabbed the baseball bat and slammed it into the trophy case with all my might. Seeing the shards of glass and the broken trophy pieces flying across the room caused a small smile to form on my face. It was as if a fire was ignited within me and I wanted to it again.

In the corner of my eye, I saw a glare from the lights on his 70-inch TV. I decided that it was going to be my next victim. I channeled my inner Tim Anderson and swung the bat. Immediately, it fell from the wall and came crashing down on the floor.

How could someone claim that they love me but treat me this way? How could he even lift his hand to me? Was I not good enough? Was there something that I did? What did I do to deserve this? With each question asked, the bat connected to something important to him.

"Karma Jonet White! What the hell are you doing?" Oya yelled out snapping me back into reality.

Taking a minute, I looked around the room and saw the damage that I had done. The room was in complete and utter disarray.

"Girl you did a number on this damn place," she stated while shaking her head. "Did it make you feel better?" She leaned against the wall and folded her arms.

She looked me in my eyes and knew that this was something that I needed to do. Granted it wasn't the best way to release my frustrations, but I knew it was going to make me feel better, and I knew that she wasn't going to judge me.

"Well then, if you're gonna fuck up some shit why not hit him where it hurts?" She gave me an evil grin and walked up the stairs. I didn't know what was about to happen, but I could only imagine. Knowing Oya, she was about to set some shit off.

An hour later, his house was a complete and utter mess.

CHAPTER FIVE
OYA ZAIRE

OKAY, I know that we may have gone a little overboard with what we did to Zo's house, but I don't regret anything we did. That piece of shit deserves everything that's coming to him. We finished packing up the U-Haul and began our journey to Ms. Rose's house.

An hour and a half later, we made it, and we were standing outside absolutely amazed. This house was nothing short of a dream. I'm not new to the finer things in life, but this was shocking. The house was beautiful, modern, and nicely kept. I know that she said her grandson purchased the house for her, but I needed to know what he did for a living.

Karma must have had the same thought because her eyes got big as she stood and admired the view. Rose must have been watching us because she pulled open the front door and ran out to hug us.

"Where have y'all been? I was expecting you an hour ago! Is everything okay?" We looked at her and shook our heads yes. She placed her hands on her hips and gave us a knowing look. "Mhmm, I just bet it is."

"We had to um, rearrange some furniture," I said while Karma snickered.

"Now why y'all go and mess up that man's house? I mean the

triflin' bastard deserves it, but there are other ways to get back at someone. Anywho, what's done is done. Now come on and let me show you around." She grabbed Karma's hand and showed us into the house.

"We'll start unloading the truck later when my grandson gets here." Rose's house was absolutely breathtaking. It was simple, yet it was warm and inviting. The décor was carefully picked out, and nothing was out of place.

"Mama Rose, this is beautiful! Who designed this house?" I asked while taking in everything that was in front of me.

"My grandson had some fancy designer try to come in here and do this place, but I wasn't having it. I'm the one that has to look at it every day, so why would I let someone else bring their vision to life. This was all too much for me at first, but then I decided to embrace it, and now I love it." She smiled.

"My grandson has been a blessing to me, so I figured why not be a blessing to someone else. That's when Karma came into my ER. Something about her made me want to help her. It seems like she's been through a lot and needed to catch a break in this cold world." She looked at Karma and smiled while continuing to show off her house.

"Well, Mama Rose, I just want you to know that we appreciate you more than you'll ever know," I kissed her cheek, and she shooed me off.

"Come on now, enough with all the mushiness. Let me show you Karma's part of the house."

Mama Rose was out doing herself. Karma's section of this massive ass house was beautiful and spacious. They were going to need walkie-talkies to communicate with each other. She didn't want or need for anything else. However, unfortunately, as Rose said, it wasn't finished just yet. The walls needed to be painted, and the carpet had to be laid. Hopefully, that wouldn't take too much time. For now, Karma would stay in one of the guest rooms that were already furnished.

CHAPTER SIX
KARMA WHITE

LAST NIGHT OYA stayed and helped me get settled. Things were going to be different from here on out, and I just wanted a little sense of normalcy in my life. The only thing normal was the love Oya was showing me. I loved my best friend with everything in me. She stayed until her boyfriend, Mase, started blowing up her phone. I didn't want to cause any more problems in their relationship, so I advised her to go home. It took a little bit of a push, but eventually, she kissed me goodbye, and I drifted off to sleep.

This morning I woke up to only a little discomfort and that was a good thing. The bed in the guest bedroom was something out of a dream. It felt so much better than being in the cold, hard hospital bed. Ms. Rose thought she was being slick, but I could hear her come in at different times throughout the night to check on me. One time, she even held her finger to my nose to make sure that I was still breathing.

The morning sun was shining brightly through the curtains, and I could tell that it was going to be a good day. Today was the first day of the rest of my life. I could sit here and wallow in my sorrows, or I could make something out of myself. The rumbling in my stomach caused me to come back to reality for a brief second. Before I went out to conquer the world, I needed to find something to put on my stomach.

As I walked into the kitchen, I was met with someone sitting on the island with a newspaper covering their face. I didn't think people still read those. This wasn't my home, so I decided to mind my business.

"Rose made a protein drink for you. It's on the counter. Drink it and then get dressed in something comfortable," he stated.

The voice was deep, and it captivated my attention as soon as I heard it, but the words that came along with it caused me to whip my head around so quickly that I became a little dazed. Who was he talking to?

"Take the drink and drink it. Don't have me tell you again," he stated.

Whoever this was had me fucked up, and I swear I wish that I didn't have these damn wires in my mouth. So instead of listening to what he was telling me, I walked over to him and snatched the paper out of his hands. Seeing his face caused me to gasp while stepping back and hitting my back against the wall.

The most gorgeous man ever stood in front of me. He had a low cut with waves and perfectly trimmed beard. His dark, chocolate skin looked as though the sun had kissed it, and his dark brown eyes pierced through me and caused me to cower like a high school girl with a crush.

Even with a scowl on his face, he was what I would describe as *stressful fine,* meaning that his looks alone had the potential to fuck up my life, and I didn't need any more of that. The flexing of his jaw caused me to come back to reality.

"You don't listen well, do you? Now I told you to drink the protein shake and get dressed." He jumped off the island and went to grab the drink. He slammed it on the counter and waited for my next move.

I picked up the drink and threw it in his face, not knowing what came over me. I was done with men treating me any kind of way. I didn't know who the fuck this man thought he was, but he was messing with the wrong bitch today. I slammed the glass back on the counter and went to find Rose. She needed to explain who this man was before he came up dead on her beautiful marble floor, and we all know that marble stains!

I ran to the guest room to grab the whiteboard and then went to search for Rose. I searched all over the house, but to my dismay, she was in the kitchen helping him clean up the mess. Seeing her cleaning up the mess had me rethinking my decision to splash him with it. Maybe that wasn't the best way for me to handle my anger.

"Karma, I see that you've met my grandson." *How did she know I was in the room? Her back was turned to me this whole time.* "Excuse him for being rude and not introducing himself. I would have done the same thing, so there are no apologies needed." She walked over to him and smacked him upside his head.

"Introduce yourself, you heathen. Comin' in here and barkin' orders at this girl like she knows you. You're lucky she didn't do more. Lord knows I would have busted you upside your head."

"Rose, watch those hands," he said while holding back his laugh. Even his laugh was sexy. "My bad, Karma." He walked away smiling without introducing himself. Rose caught on to it and just shook her head.

"Yeah, this is going to be good," she said while I helped her clean up the mess. "Gone ahead and do what he said. He's gonna be taking you to get some fresh air. You've been cooped up in the hospital, and I refuse to have you cooped up in here too. You won't be gone for long, so don't even try to fight me on it."

Fighting Rose was not on my agenda for the day but hanging out with an unknown man wasn't either. I was stuck between a rock and a hard place. After thinking for a little while longer, I just decided to go change into something comfortable. The fresh air wouldn't be so bad.

Once I was dressed and ready, the man with no name came downstairs in new clothes. The way the compression shirt hugged onto his body should have been a sin. Six perfect rows of muscle were staring at me. I could feel my mouth salivating. On the inside, I felt kind of bad for looking at him like he was the perfect piece of steak, but he was a sight to see.

He must have seen me drooling because he licked his lips and winked. I knew good and damn well that I shouldn't be having these thoughts, but he was making it so hard. He knew exactly what he was doing to me. Nevertheless, despite having these thoughts, he was still rude.

"So, are y'all going to stand there staring at each other or are you going to go get air? Get out so that I can cook breakfast in peace. Don't be gone for too long."

I grabbed my whiteboard off the table, and Rose grabbed my hand and gave it a little squeeze. If I didn't know any better, I think she was trying to set me up with her rude ass grandson. Together, we walked out of the door stuck in our own thoughts.

The weather outside was perfect. Summer was in full effect, and the sun was out shining brightly. I just wish that my mood matched it. For some reason, my mind drifted to that dark day, and sadness flushed over me.

"You good over there? Just write down what's wrong, and I'll try not to judge you."

I looked at him in disgust. I wanted to smack the shit out of him. How could someone so damn fine be so damn ignorant? Instead of smacking him, I punched him in his arm as playfully as possible.

"I'm fuckin' with you, ma. I don't mean any disrespect." All I could do was roll my eyes. "I know you're special because Rose doesn't bring just anyone to her crib, but just so you know, I ain't friendly. I'm doin' this on the strength of my OG."

Here I was thinking that he was going to be a nice guy but, in all actuality, he was trash just like the rest of them. I no longer wanted to be around him. In fear that I would take out all my frustrations on him, I turned around and went back to the house. He didn't put up a fight either.

After a few minutes, I had made it back to Ms. Rose's house. I was completely over the man who still hasn't told me his name. He was rude, and I didn't need that negativity in my life. I have enough shit going on, and I don't need him adding to it. The shit with Zo was one thing, but I wasn't going to take it from someone I barely knew. Walking in the door, I slammed it shut and went to the guest bedroom.

"I see my grandson has made a good first impression," Rose said as she walked into the room and sat down on my bed. "Don't mind him, sweetie. He's going to be a little rough around the edges, but he'll warm up to you eventually. But here, I brought you another protein smoothie. Let's try to keep this one in the cup."

She got up to walk out of the room, but I started writing on the whiteboard.

I don't think I'll ever like him. He's an asshole.

"Yes sweetie, he may be an asshole, but he might be the man that you need in your life. Don't count him out just yet." She winked and patted my leg.

What the hell did she mean by that? He was far from the man that I needed in my life. In all honesty, I didn't need a man in my life right now. I needed to deal with the one that's currently wreaking havoc on my life.

CHAPTER SEVEN
MANAHIL REEVES

SHORTY GOTTA LEARN to control her anger. I'm the last nigga that she needs to be fightin' with. When Rose approached me about moving her into the house, I was completely against it. I'm very protective of her, and I didn't need unknown people in her space. That's why I moved her outta the hood and into the burbs. It was a struggle at first, but finally, she gave in.

After Karma ran back to the house, I decided that I still needed a good work out. I wasn't gonna let shorty ruin my day with her bad attitude. Plus, I had some errands to run that was going to take up most of my day. I know Rose was gonna have a fit, but I could deal with that later.

Night had fallen by the time I made it back to the house. As soon as I walked in the door, I knew some shit was about to pop off. Rose was the type of person that didn't hold anything back when it came to how she was feeling.

"Manahil Maurice Reeves bring ya ugly ass in here now!" she yelled.

"Why are you doing all that hollerin' in here? And you know I ain't ugly. All the ladies love me." I winked at her, and she threw a throw pillow at me.

"Yeah, whatever, little boy. Don't bring no fast tail heffas near me, do you understand?" I'm not sure what *fast tail heffas* she was referring to because I didn't date. My job showed me not to trust people.

"Hil! Are you even listening to me? I didn't invite you over here to make it harder for that girl! You're supposed to be helping her, not placing her deeper into a shell. She needs this. She needs us."

Rose thought that it would be beneficial for Karma to chill with me, but I didn't plan on being a babysitter.

"Rose, you know you're my favorite girl in the world, right?" She raised her eyebrow and put her hands on her hips. She knew I was about to feed her some bullshit. No one could get anything past her. "I ain't about to babysit a grown ass woman. I'm good on that. My life is too hectic for her. You told me to take her outside, and that's what I did. You didn't say be nice to her."

"I'm not asking you to babysit her. I'm asking you to help her gain her strength back. Take her down to the gym or something when you're training. Show her around town and show her a good time. Help me reassure her that not all men are horrible creatures. I raised you right Hil, and I ask that you do this for me. She means something special to me, and I want to save her. You never know something more may come out of this."

Here she goes tryna set a nigga up. I didn't need a woman in my life, especially one as broken as Karma. I had plenty of other chicks to choose from if I needed to bust a nut. But, Rose was my world, and I didn't want to disappoint her. So, against my better judgment, I agreed.

Just as I was about to tell her that I agreed my phone went off.

"I got you, mama. If she puts up a fight, then I won't hesitate to leave her ass stranded in the middle of nowhere. We're gonna get that attitude right if she's gonna be fuckin' with me. But I gotta go, duty calls."

"When are you going to tell me what you do for a livin'? I know you ain't out here slangin' that dope because of what ya mama went through."

These conversations were never-ending. I walked over to her and kissed her forehead. She didn't need to know what I did for a livin'. She just needed to know that I was good at what I do.

"Rose, you know I'd never do anything dealing with that. You know I got you." She gave me a funny look, but I chose to ignore it. She wasn't gonna lecture me tonight. This wasn't the first time we had a conversation about my occupation. It was never up for discussion. The less she knew the better.

"I know you hear a nigga's stomach rumbling. You cookin' dinner tonight?" Rose couldn't resist cookin' for me.

She placed her hands on her hips and rolled her eyes. This was a song and dance that we've done time and time again. She wanted to say no, but she knew that she couldn't.

"I swear your ugly ass makes me sick. Now I gotta go to the store and get what I need. You want your favorite?" Of course, I wanted my favorite. OG threw down in the kitchen, and I'd be a fool to turn it down.

"I'll place it in the oven if you're not back before I leave for work. I know you're gonna be out late." She patted my chest and started to walk away, but I grabbed her arm. I gave her a hug, placed a kiss on her cheek, and ran out the door.

My job wasn't anything normal, but it paid the bills. If Rose found out what I did for a living, she would lose her shit. I lost my mom in my teen years to drugs, so I refused to go down that route and poison people with the very thing that killed her. Rose took in Shanice and me because my pops was nowhere to be found and we had nowhere to go. She was heaven sent, but it was tough going from caring for no one to caring for two growing children. She barely had enough to make ends meet before us. And with us in her house, it just put a deeper strain on her pockets.

When I got out of school, I would go to the local corner stores and barbershops to see if they had any little jobs that I could do to help put money in Rose's pockets. I lucked up when I started working for Old Man Green. He owned a liquor store and let me help him for a little change. I'm almost positive that I shouldn't have been in there in the first place, but he was good in the street, so no one bothered him.

One day while I was minding my business sweeping the floor when two men walked in that I'd never seen before. I'd been working here for a while, and I knew most of the people that walked in and out of here. These two were new that it piqued my interests. They carried two large briefcases and sat them on top of the counter. Old Man Green turned the open sign to closed and looked my way. No words needed to be said. He was going to handle some business that was none of my business. I just continued to stock the shelves so that I could get outta there and get home to Shanice and Rose.

About twenty minutes later, they came from the back and left with nothing. One good thing that I had going for me is that I was very observant. Not much bullshit could get past me, but what Green did wasn't my business. He just went to the door and turned the sign back to open. I wasn't the brightest bulb in the chandelier, but if I had to guess, Mr. Green just did a deal of some sort, and most likely the shit was illegal. It wasn't any of my business, and the only thing that mattered to me right now was finishing up, getting paid, and heading home.

When the job was complete, I went to collect my money, but Green wasn't at the front of the store anymore. His office door was closed, so I knocked, and it slightly opened on its own. On the other side of the door, Old Man Green stood staring at some of the nicest guns that I had ever seen. They were fresh off the assembly line. I didn't know that I was staring at them until he started talking and invited me over to look at them.

He also told me that I could pick it up, but I knew better than to touch them and get my fingerprints on them. I was nobody's fool. He continued talking about them, and every day after that, he would talk to me about the different types of guns that were out there.

Soon after that, I knew damn near everything there was to know about guns. Then things rapidly progressed to me learning how to shoot, and then things took a completely different turn. The same guys that I saw that night in the store approached Old Man Green and me with a proposition. They had heard from Green that I was good at shooting, and they needed someone on their team. I had no clue what kind of team they were talking about, but it involved more money than I was currently seeing, so I was down. My dumb ass didn't ask questions and found myself being a paid fuckin' assassin. Yeah, I know it's hard to believe, but it is what it is. Those men gave me an opportunity to feed my family, and I don't regret my decision at all. I've been working for Hassim and Hassan for over ten years, and I don't see myself stopping anytime soon.

CHAPTER EIGHT
KARMA WHITE

"KARMA, why do you continue to disobey me? I'm the only one in this fucked up ass world that loves you. Don't you see that? Your own mother left you, and your father knows nothing about you! Your best friend chose her relationship over you. No one gives a damn about you! You're worthless without me. I pulled you out from the shadows and turned you into the woman you are today. Without me and my money, you are nothing, absolutely nothing! You should be thanking me!"

The menacing laugh that escaped his lips caused a shiver to travel up my spine. Fear had now set in, but I wasn't going to go out like this again.

"Zo, please just stop it! You're crazy, and I'm done with you!"

The whites of his eyes were now bloodshot red, and his eyelids had formed into tiny slits. I tried to run, but my legs wouldn't move. The only thing I could do was brace myself for the beating that was about to take place.

The impact from the punch in my nightmare caused me to wake up out of my sleep dripping sweat and breathing heavily. I hated when I could feel the pain in my dreams. Looking at my phone, I noticed that the time read 2:15 *a.m.* At this point, I knew I wasn't going to be able to go back to sleep any time soon.

Since I was a little girl, whenever I had a bad dream, I would find something else to do before I went back to sleep. Otherwise, I would end up right where I left off in the dream. So, to distract myself, I decided to roam around the house.

While in the kitchen grabbing some water, I heard music coming from the basement. Now I know good and damn well that Rose wasn't here because she was currently working the overnight shift. My curiosity got the best of me, and I decided to see who was down there.

The sounds of Future got louder and louder as I made my way down the long dimly lit corridor. When I arrived at the door, I was pleasantly surprised to see *him*. Rose had a state-of-the-art gym down here, and I now know that it wasn't for *her* as much as it was for *him*.

He was currently doing reps on the bench press, and I was in awe. The strength that he was exhibiting was enough to make a girl weak at the knees. The veins popping out on his forearms had to be one of the sexiest things I'd ever seen. The way the sweat dripped off of him had me squeezing my legs together to stop the throbbing sensation that was taking place. My mind wandered to a lustful place as I thought about him wrapping me up in his arms and kissing me deeply.

As I daydreamed, I lost my balance and knocked over the trashcan by the door. He dropped the barbell back on the stand and now had a gun pointed in my direction.

"Didn't anyone teach you how to make your presence known when you walk into a room? Speak next time you creep ya ass in here!" His voice boomed throughout the room and caused me to drop my water and whimper in fear.

Also, the fact that he was holding a gun pointed my way didn't make it any better. I went to open my mouth to apologize, but the wires prevented me from doing that. So, I nodded and ran back upstairs without even cleaning up my mess. I would take care of it when he wasn't around.

When I reached my room, all I could do was jump into the bed and cry. Why did everyone hate me so much? What did I do to deserve this? I didn't mean to creep on him. I just needed to know who else was in the house.

As I lay in bed crying, I could hear my room door open. My back was towards it, but I could smell the sweat that saturated his body.

"Look, Karma," he paused for a moment, and I could hear him pulling up a chair, "I apologize. I didn't mean to yell at you, but you need to know that I'm not the type of nigga to be sneakin' up on. You almost got shot today, and I don't want Rose fuckin' me up for accidentally puttin' a bullet into you." I could hear him sigh heavily, but honestly, I was still too scared to do anything.

"Kay, turn around and look at me."

The room light came on, and with my arms, I shielded my eyes from the brightness. He came over, removed them, and stared at me with an intense gaze. The gaze wasn't what grabbed my attention. It was the feeling that I felt with my arms in his hands. The skin-to-skin contact was making my heart beat rapidly.

We stared at each other for a few moments, and then an image popped into my head. He must have felt what I felt because he quickly released my arms and took a few steps back. Our eyes never left each other, but something about this look was familiar to me. I had seen those eyes before, but I just couldn't figure out from where.

"Manahil Reeves," flowed out of his mouth and then he turned to walk out of the room.

We were making progress, and at least I knew his name now. I threw a pillow at him to get his attention. I needed to ask him a question. He stopped walking and faced me with his arms folded. I scribbled on my whiteboard and turned it towards him.

Can you teach me how to shoot? He shook his head *no* and walked out of the door.

A Few Weeks Later

Things have been going better than I expected. The part of the house that Rose had set up for me was better than I could have ever expected. She didn't have to do any of this for me, but I'm thankful she did. I knew that I wasn't going to stay here forever, but for the time being, I was going to embrace it. She even summoned Manahil to come, and he moved everything into my room. He and I haven't really communicated since the night that I saw him in the gym. I found myself going into the gym in hopes of seeing him, but as fate would have it, our paths never crossed.

Besides everything *not* going on between Hil and me, Rose had been helping me tremendously with my healing process. And today, I got the wiring removed from my jaws. It was a bittersweet feeling, but I am excited to hear my own voice again. I decided to not tell anyone about it and just surprise them. My support system had been amazing throughout this process, and I don't know where I would be without them.

Oya had been in the shop all day working like a slave. So, I knew she would be my first stop. I also figured that I would get a quick wash and blow dry while I was there. Why not kill two birds with one stone?

Pulling up to the shop, I took a deep breath and exited the car. For some reason I was nervous, but seeing her smile from the other side of the window was enough to keep my spirits up. The door chimed when I walked in, and all eyes landed on me. Even though Chicago is a large city, everyone knew your business whether you liked it or not. On a normal day, Oya's shop was a place of peace, serenity, and a no gossip zone, but today was different. I could hear the whispers, and I could only imagine what they were saying.

Since the incident, I've been flying under the radar. Before I met Lorenzo, no one knew me, and I was fine with that. However, once I got with Chicago's most eligible bachelor, everyone knew my face and name. I'm sure a thousand rumors were going around about me and why I suddenly "disappeared", but I didn't care.

The police were still investigating the incidents, so they kept in contact with me to see if I had any information about who did this.

However, I continued to tell them no. One of these days, I was going to be better, faster, and stronger. He won't get the best of me ever again.

As I walked towards Oya's station in the back, the whispers continued. A few months ago, I would cower and hide my face, but not today. Today I held my head high and kept strutting. They wouldn't be looking at me like this if they knew what I had been through.

"Kay! How are you feeling today?" she asked while she curled her client's hair. "Wait, where's your whiteboard? How are we supposed to communicate?"

"I don't need it anymore," I said as confidently as possible without laughing. The look on her face was priceless, and I wish I had taken a picture.

"Oya, don't burn her hair!" She dropped the curling iron and tears formed in her eyes. She ran over to me and damn near knocked me down.

"Oh my gosh! When did you get your wires taken out? Why didn't you tell me? I would have cleared my schedule to go with you! It feels so good to hear the sound of your voice. Aw, bestie I missed your voice!"

"I wanted to surprise everyone. You guys have been amazing during this process, and I wanted to show you that I'm gonna be good."

The two of us were now ugly crying in the shop, so Oya had her assistant finish up her client while we went back to her office.

"Wow, it feels so good to hear you talk. How are you feeling? Does it feel funny?" She fired off question after question, but it was understandable. It had been almost three months since she heard me speak. Come to think about it, the last time that she heard my voice was the night of the incident.

"My jaw still feels a little weird, but I'm happy that I don't have to write down everything anymore. I just wanted to be able to finally say thank you for saving my life. Without you answering that phone call I would have died. Oya, thank you, and I love you." The tears were falling as we were hugging. "Come on, stop crying. You're going to ruin your make up."

As soon as I said that, Oya dried up her tears and checked her makeup in the mirror on her desk.

"Now that the tears are dried, can you wash, and blow dry me?" I batted my eyes even though we both know she would never say no to me.

"Go to the bowl and let Lisa shampoo and condition you while I fix my makeup." She chuckled as I kissed her cheek.

CHAPTER NINE
OYA ZAIRE

KNOWING that my girl was going to be just fine brought tears to my eyes. I know for a fact that my girl is a fuckin' fighter, and I couldn't be prouder. She didn't let this set her back one bit.

She was currently sitting in my chair getting her hair blow-dried and living that editor life. Just watching her bounce back and get right back into work amazed me. Her situation had formed her into this strong boss ass woman, and she was a force to be reckoned with.

While I was straightening her hair, chatter from the women in the shop caused me to look up. An all-black Jeep Wrangler with icy ass rims and the doors off the hinges had pulled up to in front of the shop. I just laughed as I watched the women fix themselves up as this fine man made his way into the shop. It was cute how they even thought they stood a chance. As he made his way towards the back where I was, we connected eyes, and my heart fluttered as he licked his lips and stopped in front of me.

"Sup," he said while wrapping his arm around my waist and pulling me close to him.

"Hey handsome, how are you today?" I said in between kisses.

Mayson, also known around the streets as Mase, was my boyfriend for the past two years, and my life with him was good, but also a rollercoaster ride. We had our ups and downs just like every other relationship. Nevertheless, we continued to fight for our love even when times got hard. That's what set us above the rest.

"Sup Kay, how you feelin'?" He hit her with a head nod.

"Hey," she said dryly while not looking up from her laptop. Mase took off his sunglasses and took a step back.

"Oh shit, look who's back in commission. That's what's up. I'm glad you're talkin' again." He turned his attention to me without any further conversation with her. Mase and Kay didn't have the best relationship. She believed that I was too good for him and that he was up to no good.

It's no secret that Mase cheated on me a few months ago, but we worked out our issues, and we're moving past it.

"Let me finish her up, and then we can get outta here." He kissed me and went back to his truck.

"Aww, aren't you guys cute," Karma said sarcastically.

"Okay, now I wish you still had your wires in that smart mouth." I popped her in the head with the comb, and we shared a laugh.

"So, where are you guys headed for the afternoon?" she asked.

"I'm not sure. He said he only had a couple of things planned, but other than that we're gonna wing it. What about you?"

"I hadn't really thought about doing anything. I'm just happy to have my wires out. I'm gonna head back to the house, talk with Rose for a little bit, and then probably work out."

I had to admit it, Kay had been in the gym an awful lot lately, and her body was everything. She was now toned, slim, and thick in all the right places. My girl's ass was sitting right in these jeans, and I couldn't be prouder. I needed to take a few pointers from her. It wasn't like I was big, but I could use a little toning if I do say so myself. Nonetheless, she looked damn good. I just wished she would embrace her beauty and be the bombshell she is.

I hate that Lorenzo had broken her confidence down to a fraction.

Before she met him, she was already a shy girl. However, when they started dating, he made her as insecure as humanly possible. Eventually, she'll embrace her beauty, and when that day comes, I'll be right there hyping her up.

"Well, I'm done," I stated while I sprayed her hair.

I'd flat ironed her big curly hair bone straight with a sleek middle part, and it was sitting in the middle of her back. She got up from the seat and admired herself in the mirror.

"Thanks, Ya," she said as she tried to slip some money in my hand, but I refused. Karma always tried to pay me, but I'll never allow it. "Ugh, I hate when you do that. Get out of here and enjoy your evening with Mase." We kissed each other goodbye and went our separate ways.

"Where are we headed, babe?" I asked eagerly.

We had been in the car for about fifteen minutes cursing down Chicago's infamous Lake Shore Drive. The wind was blowing through my hair, and the sun was shining brightly on us. It was damn near the perfect afternoon.

"We're gonna chill and go with the flow," he said while showing off that killer smile.

"You know I love you, right?" he said as he placed his hand on my thigh.

"Yeah, I know you do. I love you too." I found myself gushing over him. The feelings he gave me would never get old.

While we cruised, I closed my eyes and thought about where I currently was in my life. I was with the man of my dreams, my best friend was getting better by the day, and business was booming. There was so much more that I could ask for like marriage and babies, but they would come eventually. At this point in my life, I learned just to go with the flow. If it's meant to be, then baby it'll be.

The car had come to a stop, so I opened my eyes to see that we were pulling up to one of my favorite shopping centers. I didn't plan on shopping today, but I wasn't going to object to it either.

Darkness started falling on us as we waited for the clerk to wrap up our last items. A few hours and a couple of thousand dollars later, Mase and I were done tearing up the mall. One would think that I was the one that spent the most money, but they were sadly mistaken. Mase had a sneaker habit that was out of control. His house has two walk-in closets dedicated for just sneakers. Who on God's green earth needed that many pairs of shoes and you only had two feet? It didn't make sense, but I dare not call him out on it.

Once the bags were in the car, the only thing on my mind was food. I typically worked long hours and barely had any time to eat, so if the next thing on our agenda wasn't getting some food, then we were going to have some issues. I ain't nice when I'm hungry.

"Sit back, Oya. I can hear ya stomach," he smacked his lips playfully and mushed my leg. "Actin' like you haven't eaten in days."

"Don't get fucked up Mase, but you know me so well." The car came to a stop, and the valet came over to help me out, but Mase shut that down quick. The guy got the hint and took a few steps back.

"My bad man, I was just trying to help the young lady out of the car, but I see you. Respect," he said as Mase gave him the keys.

"'Preciate it youngin', but yeah I got her, trust me. Just make sure my shit comes back in one piece." They slapped hands, and we continued into the restaurant.

We were quickly seated by the hostess, and our waitress came over quickly to take our orders. She had her head down when she approached the table and started talking.

"Welcome to Capital Grille, my name is Mya, can I get you all started with—" she picked her head up and looked at me and then

Mase. The pen and piece of paper that occupied her hand had now fallen to the floor. He looked up from his menu and then the air around us started to thicken as the two of them began having a staring contest.

"*Ahem, ahem,*" I cleared my throat trying to get their attention, but neither budged.

The looks on their faces let me know that this wasn't their first time seeing each other, making this encounter even more awkward. Uncertainty began setting in for me, and that was something that I didn't often do. I needed to know what the hell was going on, and I needed to know it right now. As soon as I was about to open my mouth, she decided to open hers.

"I-I'm sorry, let me go get you all another waiter." That was the only thing that I agreed with right about now. She began to walk off, but Mase thought that opening his mouth was the best thing to do at this moment.

"Mya, come back," his voice was low as he commanded her to come back.

Someone needed to start talking soon, or I was bound to act a fool in this nice ass restaurant. Mya walked back to the table and stood in front of him with her head down. Whatever hold he had on her was scary, to say the least.

"Look at me," he said, and in an instant her head raised, and she looked him directly in his menacing, dark brown eyes.

"This is what you're doing now?" She nodded and went right back to holding her head down.

"Look at me when I'm talking to you." Once again, she followed his command and held her head up.

"Monsieur, please let me expl—" she tried to please with him, but he held his hand up cutting her off. She immediately closed her mouth and looked down at her feet.

"Oh, y'all got me fucked up. Somebody better get to talkin' 'fore I get to shootin'," I said as I slammed my little black nine on the table.

These two had lost their minds if they thought that I was going to sit here while they did this little song and dance. Neither of them moved an inch. It was as if they were talking without saying any words. I pulled my phone out and ordered an Uber before I found myself sitting in Cook County Jail for premeditated murder.

My phone alerted me that my Uber was outside, so I kindly excused myself from the table and began walking towards the front. Mase called out for me, but his ass had yet to get up from that damn table. I rarely followed instructions because I had multiple problems with authority. With everything that just transpired between them, it confirmed that Mya was someone from his not so distant past. Once again, men were showing me that they weren't shit.

"Hi, Oya?" the Uber driver asked.

"Yes, that's me. Let's go, before you witness me catching a case." I placed my shades on and silently cried as he pulled off.

"Are you okay back there?" The Uber driver was looking at me through the mirror. I had my head placed against the window, so I thought his view of me was obstructed, but I guess I was wrong.

"Yes, I'm fine thank you for asking," I said while struggling to keep my composure. He kept trying to make small talk with me, but I just wanted to be left alone in my thoughts.

"You want me to beat him up?" he asked as I gave a small chuckle.

"No thank you. Wait, why do you think that I'm crying over a man?"

"The only time I see pretty women like you cry is when a man had fucked up in some way. One would assume you were crying because you were sad, but see I'm smarter than that," he stated while tapping his forehead with his index finger. "You're crying because you want to lay hands on him and whoever else pissed you off. You seem like the type of woman that cries when you're mad because you don't want to go to jail. Am I right?"

I hated to admit it, but he was absolutely right. Whenever I was mad beyond belief, I would cry. I don't know why I did this, but it's been a trait of mine since I was a little girl. To avoid answering his question I decided just to laugh it off while wiping away the rest of the tears.

"Yeah, I thought so. Like I said, if you need me to beat him up I will."

He looked at me again, and I couldn't help but take in his facial features. He was a decent looking guy with a low cut fade with a struggle beard to match. He wasn't the most handsome man that I had seen in my life, but he wasn't sore on the eyes if you know what I mean. The vibes that he was giving off would end up meaning more to me than looks. However, when he smiled, it took away my breath. Here he was showing off a set of perfectly white teeth and then he had the nerve to wink at me. I knew right then that I needed to look away, but I couldn't pull my eyes away from the mirror. Our gaze lasted much longer than it should have.

"You might want to watch the road instead of watching me," I finally found my words a few moments into our stare down.

"I'm good, love. Chicago is my city and I know what I'm doing. You just make sure that this is your last time crying over him. Listen to whatever he has to say, and if you feel that it's bullshit, then leave him. Listen to how he explains himself. You'll be able to tell if he's on bullshit or not. If he's on bullshit, then call me, and I'll take you anywhere you want to go. If I don't hear from you, then I know that everything with you is good." He was no longer looking in the mirror, and I didn't know how to feel about that.

"Why are you being so nice to me?" I needed to know why he felt the need to give me this advice and why he was willing to fight for a woman he knew nothing about.

"As I said before, a pretty strong woman like yourself should not be crying. I felt your vibe when you got in my car. If you need me, I'll be your Superman and come rescue you," he said with a straight face.

As soon as I was about to open my mouth, I noticed that we had pulled in front of my building. He hit the locks as I placed my hand on the door handle.

"I'm not Lois Lane, so I don't need you to be my Superman.

Thank you for the ride umm..." I didn't even have his name. "I'm sorry. I don't know your name." I fumbled to pull my phone out of my purse so that I could read his name off of the app.

"It's Nix," he stated.

"What kind of name is that? Is that short for Nixon?" I thought I was asking myself these questions, but it seems as though I said it aloud.

"What kind of name is Oya?" He fired back. "But no, it's just Nix."

"Touché. Well, thank you for the ride, Nix. I hope you have a great night. Goodbye." I exited the car and began walking to my door, but the sound of his window rolling down made me stop in my tracks.

"Don't say goodbye to me, Oya. Goodbye means that you don't intend to see me again. I was serious about what I said. If he doesn't come correct, then call me. I'll always answer for you. See ya later, Oya."

"This is goodbye, Nix. Maybe in another lifetime but not this one." With those words, I walked into my apartment building and got on the elevator.

I didn't want to look at the door, but my eyes had other plans. I looked up, and Nix was still hanging on the window showing off that perfect smile. The one time I didn't want the elevator doors to close quickly, they did, and in a flash, he was gone.

Walking into my apartment, the events of the night started to flood back into the forefront of my mind. What the hell was going on with my man? Who was the woman from the restaurant? I needed answers, and I'd be damned if I didn't get them. Mase had some explaining to do.

In due time I would get my answers, but for now, I was going to shower and find a good book to read. That combination was sure to calm me down and rationalize what happened today.

As soon as I was about to step into the steaming hot shower my phone dinged. I was going to ignore it, but then it dinged again, and then it dinged two more times. If it was Mase, then I was going to lose my damn mind.

630-555-1908: *Again, it's never 'goodbye' Queen. It's 'see ya later'.*

630-555-1908: *Nix*

630-555-1908: *Lock it in*

630-555-1908: *Attachment Image:* ı

This man was really feeling himself with these messages. He'd sent me a selfie showing off that perfect ass smile. Ugh. I had half a mind to report him to Uber for abusing his power like this, but something in me wasn't letting Mr. Nix go. My shower water was going to get cold if I kept dealing with this man.

Me: *You know this is an abuse of power, right?*

As soon I sent the message, this fool was calling my phone. I went back and forth for about fifteen seconds on whether I should answer this phone call or just leave it be. Against my better judgment, I answered it.

"Hello," it came out like a whisper, and I had no clue why.

"Hello to you too, Ms. Oya." The way his voice sounded on the phone was intoxicating. Nix was going to be a problem in my life, and I wasn't sure that I wanted this to end.

CHAPTER TEN
MAYSON WHITE

THINGS AT DINNER with Oya were not supposed to go down like that. Seeing Mya had thrown me completely off my square and I knew that I had a lot of fuckin' explaining to do. Oya knew nothing about Mya, and I never wanted Oya to know about her. Up until that moment, I hadn't seen Mya in about five years.

Mya was the only female that I allowed in my heart, and then one day she just up and left like a thief in the night. She had the nerve to pack her shit and leave a "Dear John" letter next to my empty safe. The money she stole from me didn't mean anything to me. It was the fact that I'd asked her time and time again if this was what she wanted, and every time she assured me that it was.

Our relationship was a little unconventional, but she knew what it was from the beginning. We had an understanding, and she agreed with it. However, when my feelings started to get involved, it's like she had completely shut out the idea of being the main lady in my life. One would describe our relationship to be like a *Fifty Shades of Grey* type shit, but that's what worked for us. Never did I think that my feelings for Mya would grow, but they did.

As my love for her grew, she became more distant. She wasn't interested in doin' the things we had become accustomed to, and I'm the type of person that hates change when I don't initiate it. Mya was sneaky before I fell in love with her, but once she found out how I truly felt, it was as if she became a completely different person. The night she left my crib with my money was the day that she had signed her death wish, or so I thought. I had planned every detail when it came to killin' her, but seeing her in front of me right now had me stuck. Time stood still, and I couldn't breathe.

I could see Ya losing her shit little by little, but I couldn't control my actions even if I tried. Mya was the only woman that had this type of hold on me. I was a sucker for her pretty pecan colored skin, blonde curly tresses with dark brown roots, and a body that could make this grown man cry. Her piercing gray eyes stared at me with such intensity that I had to look away.

"Have a seat," I instructed her as I kicked the chair that was in front of her.

"Monsieur, I can't sit down. I'll lose my job if I sit down," she said just above a whisper.

Mya was of African American and French descent. Typically, we would bounce between speaking English and French. To her I was *Monsieur,* and to me she was *Mademoiselle.*

"Mademoiselle, you need to be worried about losing your life instead of this job. Now have a seat."

Reluctantly she sat down with her hands in her lap as she twirled her thumbs. That was something she did when she was nervous. Mya seemed to have forgotten that I knew everything about her. Being a dominant, I needed to know her likes and dislikes and what made her laugh what made her cry. After finding out almost everything about her is when I started to fall in love. It was as if she was the Ying to my Yang.

"Why'd you leave, Mya?" I tried not to show my frustrations, but I'm sure I was wearing it on my face.

"Our relationship was going in a direction that I wasn't ready for at that time. I was young and stupid, but it was never my intentions hurt you. You've got to believe that. My decision to leave haunts me each and every day."

What Mya didn't know was that I knew she could spit mean game. She put on this innocent act like she regretted her decision, but I knew better, once a snake always a snake.

"Mayson," she gasped as soon as the word left her mouth, and those gray eyes grew as wide as the saucers on the table. She knew better than to call me Mayson. Calling me by given name was a privilege she lost a long fuckin' time ago.

"YOU DON'T GET TO CALL ME THAT!" My anger had gotten the best of me as my voice echoed throughout the restaurant. It brought attention to me, and that was something that I hated to say the least. "You're going to be leaving here with me. Do you understand?"

If I flexed my jaw anymore, I would have broken a few teeth. Mya went to open her mouth in protest, but the look that was plastered on my face informed her that it wasn't up for debate.

"I'm not going to fight you, Monsieur. Just let me tell my manager that I have to go." She looked at me again with those emerald eyes, and my heart started to soften for her. However, if Mya thought that I was the same man that she fucked with five years ago, she had another thing coming.

"Bring ya manager here, Mya. I'll tell him my damn self."

She nodded and got up from the table, but before she could fully stand, I grabbed her by the knee and gave it a good squeeze.

"Don't play me. I let you get away with your life once. You won't make it far a second time."

After a few minutes, she brought over a short, stubby looking guy who she introduced as her manager. He tried to put up a fight, but when I put a band on the table, his demeanor changed quickly. He allowed Mya to leave with no hesitation. I had given her three minutes to grab her shit and meet me outside. She was out front in less time than that. I hated bringing out this side of me, but it was necessary when it came to a chick like her. Here I was toying back and forth with Mya that I didn't even realize that Oya had bounced. I had fucked up royally, and I didn't know how I was going to fix this shit.

The same valet guy that originally took my keys was still out there. The moment he saw me with Mya, his facial expressions changed, but he didn't open his mouth to say a word. I respected the fact that he minded his damn business.

"Aye, have you been out here the whole time?" He nodded but didn't say a word.

"Did you see what happened to the woman that I came in here with?"

"Yeah, she came out here crying and then hopped in the Uber. I was gonna ask if she was good, but I learned to mind my business a long time ago." I gave him a hundred-dollar bill before he went to grab my truck.

I don't know how I was going to explain this to Oya, but right now, that was the furthest thing from my mind.

During the car ride, Mya sat with her head resting on her hand while she stared aimlessly out of the window. I had no clue what I was doing with her and why I was doing it. It was as if my body was on autopilot with her. I knew that it wouldn't be wise for me to go to my house since Oya had a key. I decided to drive to a hotel downtown and get a room for the night. I was going to get some answers out of Mya if it's the last thing I do.

"You ain't gonna say shit?"

"Monsieur, what do you want me to say? I decided that night to leave this relationship, but I don't regret it. The only thing I regret is leaving you the way that I did. You deserved much more than what I gave you, and for that, I would like to apologize." She placed her hand on my knee, and my body tensed up from the touch.

"Why didn't you want to be with me? I don't understand what I did wrong." For years, I hoped and prayed for this moment. She sat deep in thought as we arrived at the Langham Hotel and continued to think even after I checked in.

"You know this is abducting, right? I'm being held against my will," she said as she placed her purse on the side table.

Walking over to the door I held it open for her. When she didn't leave, I knew I had her right where I wanted her. Those old feelings were resurfacing, and there was no going back. I closed the door and went in search of the room service menu. I hadn't had a chance to eat at the restaurant, and my stomach was now touching my back. Mya saw that this was for real, and we weren't going anywhere any time soon. She took off her shoes and started to get comfortable. Once the shoes were off, she started to unbutton her shirt, and without my permission, my body started to react. She knew what she was doing, and I can't say that I didn't like it. Mya Elle Marchand was my drug, and I needed a hit. Things with Oya would never be the same after this.

OYA HAD me feeling so good about myself right now. She had flat ironed my hair bone straight, and I ended up going downstairs to my girl Ash to get my eyebrows done. For the first time in a long time, I felt beautiful and free. Nothing or no one could steal my joy.

While at Oya's shop, I was finally able to get some editing done. I had taken on a few side projects, and they needed to be completed pretty soon. During that time, I realized that I never grabbed my editing storage bin. This bin contained all the things that I needed to deliver the perfect edits.

As I pulled into the parking lot of my apartment building, the old feelings that I thought I suppressed were resurfacing. The memories of the simpler times in my life started to hit me harder than I had expected. I recalled the times where I would come home and sit on my cozy window seat while editing or curling up with a good book. That was before I let a man come in and change all of that for me.

My mind drifted to thoughts of just how much I've changed. Being with Lorenzo was nice, but he had started to change everything that made me who I was.

As I lay on the shower floor, I wondered how we got here. Not once in our time together had Zo ever put his hands on me. The anger that flashed in his eyes before his fist drew contact with my face was enough to scare the manliest of men.

The scolding hot water couldn't numb the pain that I was experiencing. Never in my life had I felt so low, but I refused to stay with a man that used me as a punching bag. There was nothing that he could do to turn this around. Lifting myself off the floor, I turned the water off and grabbed my towel off the rack. I needed to get out of here. Thankfully, he wasn't in the room when I got there, so I assumed he was in his man cave. I had to move now if I was going to get out of here untouched.

Quickly drying off, I ran to his master bedroom and grabbed a pair of leggings and a hoodie out of the drawer to put on. As I stepped in the closet to grab a pair of UGGS, I heard the bedroom creek open. My heart stopped beating, and fear had set in quickly.

"So, you're trying to leave me?" Hell yeah, I'm trying to leave you. That's what my soul was screaming out, but I knew that wouldn't be the smart thing to do. I needed to tread lightly.

"No," was all I managed to get out. The fear that was running through my veins was evident in my voice.

Zo sat on the bed and put his head in his hands while taking a deep breath.

"Pretty girl, I'm sorry. I don't want you to ever be afraid of me." I could hear just how sorry he was, but that didn't excuse the fact that he hit me with a closed fist. That was inexcusable.

"Zo, I need some time to think about this. You're drunk, and I'm in pain. I'm going to go to Oya's house for the night so that we can revisit this conversation with clear heads," I said with a shaky voice.

"W-why you gotta leave the house?" he asked with slurred words. The smell of scotch has now filled the room, and he absolutely reeked of it.

"Because I need some time to think and I can't think with us being in the same house. I refuse to become a punching bag for you. Please just allow me some time to think about this."

Making the mistake of turning my back was possibly the worst *thing that I could do. I had bent down to place the boot on my foot, and a hit to the back of my head caused me to fly forward into the wall.*

"You are not leaving this fuckin' house tonight, Karma." I turned around to face him, and Satan himself was in this house. "Now, I know ya ass is upset, but if you need to figure some shit out, you are gonna do that right here in this house. I don't need ya nosey ass friend in our business. It was a mistake, and I apologize. It won't fuckin' happen again."

He turned to walk away, and the tears that I had been holding in were now spilling out of my eyes.

"Get up and take ya ass to one of these guest rooms. I'll see you in the morning. If you try to leave, so help me God, I will find you and drag your ass back here by the roots of your hair. I gotta run an errand, so I'll be back. Figure out where you're sleeping tonight." He walked away and left me to cry on the closet floor.

The sound of the door being played with snapped me out of my flashback. I wiped tears from my eyes and stood like a deer in head-lights waiting for the door to fly open. I reached for my phone and realized that I didn't have it on me. I must have left it in the car. How could I have been so stupid?

Before I could answer that question, Lorenzo had come busting in the door. He looked though he hadn't slept in weeks. This was not the man that I had fallen in love with. He had to be at least fifteen pounds heavier than the last time I saw him. His eyes had deep bags under them, and the little goatee that he had on his chin had now grown into a full-fledged beard. The struggle had come and slapped him in his face hard. However, the smell of liquor caused me to stop taking in his appearance and notice that he was pissy drunk.

"I knew you'd come back here." He closed the door and tried to lock it even though he had broken the knob. He started walking towards me, and I wanted to run, but I couldn't move.

"Karma, baby, I'm so sorry. I need help controlling my anger, and I promise to get help, but baby I need you to come back home. I can't function without you."

He continued towards me, and I was finally able to step back. Unfortunately, for me, I fell back onto the couch. Zo stood in front of me, and then he kneeled in between my legs.

"Please say something," he said as he held my face in his hands. The smell that came from his mouth was like something had died inside of him. It was awful.

"I'm not coming back." He turned into a completely different person as soon as the words came out of my mouth.

"I don't understand," he said to himself while banging his fist against his head. "I've done everything right, and the one time I fuck up, she wants to act like I'm the worst thing in the world."

"You haven't fucked up just *one* time, Lorenzo!"

I'd found my voice, and I was glad that I did. Before all of this happened I would have been too afraid to stand up to him, but not anymore. I'm not going to be his punching bag any longer.

"Zo, it's been two and a half years of fuck-ups, and two and a half years of 'baby, I'm sorry' and 'pretty girl, I won't do it again'. and I'm sick of it." He hadn't moved a muscle, and it was as if he was trying to process what I said.

"Zo, you need to leave."

I moved my leg to get up, but he quickly wrapped his hands around my neck. I refused to let him get the best of me this time. It was time for me to fight back and show myself that I don't deserve this.

With everything in me, I began raining down hits on him. He was much stronger than I was, but the time that I had been spending in the gym was giving me a little hope. Unfortunately, my punches were no match for him. Therefore, I did what the women do in every movie. I looked for something to stab him with. On my coffee table sat an elephant figurine that I had purchased from Target some time ago. The tusks were extended and pointy, which made for the perfect weapon.

Zo was so focused on choking me that he didn't realize that I was reaching for the elephant. It was becoming harder and harder for me to breathe, and I needed to do this before I blacked out. I was able to get my hands on it and quickly shoved the tusk in his shoulder.

"Ahhhh! Stupid bitch! I got you. Don't even worry about it. This ain't over bitch."

While I was gasping for air, he ripped the elephant out of his arm, threw it on the floor, and ran out of the door. Hopefully, he'll realize that I'm not going down without a fight each and every time. Enough was enough.

After making a phone call to a locksmith, I waited in the apartment with a hammer in my hand until I felt it was safe enough for me to leave. Nighttime had now fallen upon me as I hopped in my car. The drive to Rose's house was long and excruciating. My neck was on fire, and I'm sure that it was going to bruise. Thankfully, Rose was still working the night shift, so I could sneak in and get this neck iced and covered up without her even knowing.

During the drive, many questions ran through my head. How did he know I was there? How long had he been waiting to make his move? Why won't he just leave me alone?

When I arrived home, Manahil was laying on the couch snoring as loud as his body would handle. It enraged me even more because he had a place to stay yet he was always here. Why was he always here? Butterflies in my stomach started to flutter, and I couldn't understand why. Yes, he's a handsome ass man, but he's obnoxious, and I didn't need that in my life. I had enough problems to deal with. I shook the thought off and began tiptoeing to my room. I hated that I had to sneak past him, but I didn't want him to see the bruises that were forming on my neck.

I thought I was being as quiet as humanly possible, but I failed. My focus was off because I was looking at this handsome ass creature and ended up running knee first into a wall.

CHAPTER TWELVE
MANAHIL REEVES

A FEW HOURS EARLIER

LATELY, I had been spending a whole lot of time here at Rose's house. I know she has her own ideas as to why I'm here, but I didn't want to hear it. Honestly, I knew it'd be some bullshit about me falling for Kay.

"Damn Rose, you got it smellin' right in here. Aye, you hooked it up."

She turned around and wiped her hands on her apron while looking me over. I had just come from doing a job, and it was as if she could sense it. We did this song and dance more than once, so I knew exactly what she was trying to do. Deciding not to feed into her actions, I walked over to the stove and started looking in the pots. She was still trying to find out what I did for a living, and it wasn't going to happen. The less she knew, the better off we were.

"Stop lookin' at me like that." I walked over to her and kissed her. As I was standing back up, she grabbed my face in her hands.

"Manahil Maurice Reeves, why is there blood on your face?" I had no clue what she was talkin' about, so I went to look in a mirror. Sure enough, I had fucked up. In all my years of doing what I do not once have, I ever slipped up like this. This shit wasn't like me by far.

"Man ma, the barber must have cut me while he was linin' me up. It's no big deal, now come on and eat."

Walking my ass to the table, I knew shit was going to go left. The shit that just flew outta my mouth was by far the dumbest shit I've ever said.

"Mmhmm," was all she said as we sat down and ate dinner.

"You sure are spending a lot of time around here since Karma moved in. Anything you want to tell me?" Rose thought she was good at reading vibes and most of the time she was, except for now.

"Nah," I wanted to look her in her eyes to reassure her that there wasn't anything going on from this end, but I found myself not being able to at her directly. The more I thought about it, the more I started to question and doubt myself. However, I refused to let Rose know what was going on. If she knew that there was an ounce of doubt in me, she was going to start digging, and I damn sure didn't need that.

"I'm only around here so much because you've let a strange woman that you met at the hospital into ya house. I'm gonna be around here until I know for a fact that you're straight and she doesn't have another agenda." I winked at Rose and stuffed my mouth with meatloaf. Hopefully, that answer would hold her off until I could shake away my uncertainty.

"Hil, that girl has been here for weeks and is no threat to me. I know the real reason why you're here, but I'm not going to push the subject, yet." I had to sit back and laugh at that one. It was no winning with Rose.

"You're hiding multiple things from me Manahil, and I don't like it. However, one of these days you're going to finally tell me what you're doing running around this city, and one of these days you'll come clean and tell me how you feel about Karma. She may have been a hot broken mess when she walked through those doors a few weeks ago, but right now, the Phoenix has risen from her ashes, and she's about to set the world ablaze. It's best you get on her good side while you can. I'm not going to preach to you about it tonight. Until then I'm gonna continue to overlook things and mind my black ass business. Just make sure you're being safe. Now I'm about to get going. Are you staying here, or are you going home?" she asked as she prepared her lunch bag for the night.

"I'm gonna crash here for a few. You know that food hit me just right. A nap is in my future. But before I do that, I'll clean up this mess."

I kissed her goodbye, cleaned up the kitchen, and laid my black ass down. The words that Rose spoke about Karma were hitting me. I didn't want to believe that I was in denial about my feelings for her, but I knew I couldn't suppress these feelings for long. Not wanting to dwell on it anymore, I laid on the couch and was out. The ringing of my phone stirred me out of my sleep, and I was pissed. I was getting some good as sleep.

"Young Hil, how's life?" Hassim asked in the phone. It caught me off guard because he rarely ever called me outside of doing a job for him.

"Sup, Sim. What do I owe the pleasure of this call?" I was straight to the point. I rarely liked keeping my phone on before a job, let alone answer a call.

"Always quick and to the point. I hear that Ms. Rose has a new visitor. How's that working out?"

I gritted my teeth at the mention of Karma. I didn't know how he knew about her or why he was even asking questions. I found myself getting upset, and I shouldn't have been.

"What does it matter to you? You know her or something?"

"Ahh, that's all I needed to know. You have a good night." He hung up without answering the question. This shit was gonna bother me until I knew why he asked about Kay.

I was already struggling to fall asleep after the call with Hassim, but the sound of something hitting a wall caused me to jump and grab my gun from under the pillow. Kay placed her hands over her mouth and gasped when she saw the moonlight flash as I held my Glock by my side. Not wanting to scare her further, I put it in the small of my back and flicked on the light.

The sight before me enraged me to the point where I could feel the smoke coming from my ears. Her eyes were bloodshot red and puffy, but the fresh set of handprints around her neck caused me to flex my jaw in anger.

"Who did it?" I asked through clenched jaws. She held her head down, but I picked that shit right back up. "Kay, tell me who the fuck did this shit." I walked over to the table and grabbed her whiteboard. I needed for her to tell me it was that fuck nigga so that I could dead his ass on sight.

"Why do you care, Manahil?" The sound of her voice had thrown me off my square. I didn't even know she got her wires removed. Her voice was soft but forceful. The pain was oozing out, and all I wanted to do was grab her and put her in my arms and let her know this shit was going to be ok.

"Kay, I'm going to ask you one last time. Who the fuck did it?"

"You know exactly who did it, my stupid ass ex-boyfriend who refuses to leave me alone. I've done everything for him, and this is how he treats me. What did I do? Why does God hate me?" She was having a mental breakdown, and I didn't know how to deal with the emotional shit, so I did what I do best.

"Where were y'all at?"

"My old apartment."

"What kinda car does he drive on a regular?"

"I'm not sure. Usually, it's his yellow Mustang GT, but he could have changed it up since the accident."

"Cool, you still got that nigga's number?" She shook her head yes and passed me her phone. There was only one nigga that was a beast with the tech that could find out what I needed to know, so I dialed him up.

"Aye Que, what's good, my nigga? Sorry for the late call but I need you to ping a location."

"No, Manahil, don't do that. It'll only make things worse, and I don't want you to get hurt." She covered her mouth when she realized what she said. No lie, it caught me off guard as well. Kay ran off to her room to avoid saying anything else to me that she wasn't ready to say.

"My bad, hold off on that info. I'll stop by and see you and Rhy tomorrow. I'll explain everything then. Let me deal with this." We ended the conversation, and I went to look for her.

She was in her bathroom examining the damage, and I couldn't do shit but shake my head. The nigga did a number on her, and I was going to make it my mission to find his ass and kill him if it's the last thing I do. I didn't know what feelings I had for Kay, but them bitches were strong enough for me to kill for her.

"Can you teach me how to shoot?" she asked shyly.

"Nah ma, you gonna have to stop wasting your free questions on stupid shit."

"Ugh, why not? What is so wrong with me wanting to know how to protect myself? Do you see this?" She pulled off her shirt exposing the damage he had done. It wasn't as bad as I thought, but they shouldn't have been there in the first place.

"These are from me not being able to defend myself. Look at me!" she yelled as she broke down on the floor. I wanted to explain everything to her, but it was a sensitive subject for me. The last person I taught to shoot a gun was my sister.

"Hil, I got this." Shanice laughed as she pointed the gun at the target. "I'm not a little girl anymore. I got this. Now step back and watch me do this."

My little sister Shanice had begged me to take her to the gun range to teach her to shoot. She was fascinated with the Marines and wanted to be just like this. The shit scared me, especially with everything going on in the world, but she was determined to become the best of the best. So, on her eighteenth birthday, I had finally given in and taught her. I wasn't sure why she felt the need for me of all people to teach her, but I couldn't deny my baby what she wanted. She was all I had and vice versa.

"Stop worrying about me and aim the gun, lil mama. Breathe and aim," I said as she fired off round after round and they were damn near

perfect. I had created a sharpshooter, and I couldn't have been prouder.

"Thank you, Hil. You are the best big brother ever!"

"Manahil! You walk around here every other day pointing a gun in my face, but now you don't want to teach me? What's so wrong with me knowing how to protect myself? Why won't you teach me?" Karma yelled.

"Because I fucking said so! That's why. Karma, damn! You don't fuckin' get it!" I didn't mean to raise my voice at her, but I just couldn't bring myself to tell her why I didn't want to do it. I found myself caring about Kay more and more each day, and I refused to teach someone else that I care about how to use a damn gun.

She pointed to the door letting me know that she didn't want me in her presence anymore, so I left out without putting up a fight. My hands were tied, and there was nothing more that I could do when it came to that situation. I hated to be this way, but I just couldn't bring myself to do it. She was gonna have to understand it.

"Que, man, thanks for comin' out here on such short notice."

Que was a longtime partner of mine. He was a beast with the tech, and he helped with some of my jobs. Whenever I needed more information, he would come through in the clutch.

"Man, you know I don't get out of bed for many people. Wifey said I got twenty minutes. Let's hurry this shit up." He handed me a folder, and I started to flip through the files.

"Damn son, she got you out here like that?" Rhyland wasn't one to play with when it came to Que. I've heard plenty of stories about the two of them, and they were down to ride for each other. That kinda love was hard to come by.

"Hell yeah, happy wife, happy life," he said while shaking his head.

"Okay tell me what I'm lookin' at?"

"I'll make this as quick as I can. The man suffers from borderline personality disorder as well as severe anxiety. His last prescription was filled about two and a half years ago."

Que had said a mouth full, and I didn't even know where to begin.

"Thanks, man, I appreciate it." We dapped each other up and went our separate ways. I had a lot to think about, and I needed to figure out where to start.

CHAPTER THIRTEEN
KARMA WHITE

THIS MAN WAS REALLY WORKING my fuckin' nerve. Who the hell did he think he was yelling at me? It was just a simple question, and he didn't have to answer me the way he did. Something is seriously wrong with him, but I didn't even want to find out. In due time, he would tell me what was wrong and until then, fuck Manahil Reeves. I'd find a way to learn how to protect myself on my own.

The pain around my neck started to intensify, so I decided just to take a shower and take some pain meds. This day was far too much for me to handle, but I would use these experiences to make me better. Lorenzo was going to get what was coming to him if that's the last thing I do. I know that I'm supposed to him forgive, but right now, I'm not in the business of forgiving.

As the water fell over my body, my heart wanted me to scream and cry out, but my mind wouldn't allow it. I'm thankful that I've been listening to my mind because my heart has been kinda stupid lately. The droplets of water beating down on my body were soothing, but still painful nonetheless. I cut the shower short and finished my nightly routine before climbing in the bed. The clock on my nightstand read 1:39 *a.m.,* and I was in disbelief. Today was yet another day from hell, and I just wanted to start seeing better days.

The feeling of my bed sinking in on one side caused my eyes to shoot open in fear, but my body didn't move. That is until a strong arm found its way around my waist and instantly my body relaxed beneath it. It was as if my body knew that it was him. We had never been this close to one another, and for the life of me, I couldn't understand why we were.

"I know you think I'm some rude ass nigga, but I'm far from it. Before you open your mouth, let me tell you a few things about me. Can you do that? If you can't do that, then I'll walk my ass out of this room and not come back." I gave him a simple nod, and he proceeded to talk.

"The last person that I taught to shoot was my little sister, Shanice. All she ever wanted in life was to be a badass Marine. She ate, slept, and breathed that shit. Never once in my life had I seen her playing with Barbie dolls. For Christmas, she would always ask for war dolls and shit, you know, like GI Joe's. She was in love with movies surrounding assassins and snipers. Not once did we try to change her views because we loved the fact that she was passionate about something."

He paused and took a deep, shaky breath, and I inhaled with him, but I was holding onto mine. Whatever he was about to tell me wasn't going to be a happy ending.

"For years and years, Shanice begged me to teach her to shoot or take her to a gun range. My little sis was my world, and all I ever wanted to do was make her happy. I had a rough upbringing, and all I wanted to do was keep her from facing the same hardships that I had. So, I hustled hard to make sure she had what she wanted, but most importantly what she needed. Seeing as though she was following her dreams, I finally caved in and taught her.

"What I didn't know she was battling some of her own issues. She didn't even feel comfortable telling me that shit, Kay."

His labored breathing let me know that he was on the verge of breaking down. I tried to turn to face him, but his hold on me was too strong.

"What happened to her?" Honestly, I was terrified of what was going to come out of his mouth. It's obvious that it was heartbreaking, so I placed my hand on top of his and intertwined our fingers.

"She decided to eat a bullet all because of a broken heart. That shit fucked me up to the core. It fucked me up to the point that I question if I ever want to love again. Who wants love when it can make you do shit like that?"

"Hil, you can't be afraid to love because of what someone else went through—"

"But that's the thing, Kay. She didn't even feel comfortable telling me what was going on with her. My own sister didn't even want to tell me that she was suffering from a broken heart. What kinda love is that?"

He was slowly breaking down behind me, and I didn't know whether to let him do this on his own or should I turn around and console him. Against my better judgment, I squirmed to face him while keeping his massive arm around me. It felt too good to remove. I placed my hands on his face and placed his forehead on mine. Tears slid down the sides of my thumbs, and I gently wiped them away.

"Hil, some things are just too hard to discuss, especially when it involves your loved ones. Time and time again, I wanted to tell Oya what was going on, but I could never bring myself to do it. I was ashamed of what my life had become. Ashamed of letting the man that claimed he loved me beat me like I was his sparring partner."

Just hearing myself talk about it caused a wave of sadness to rush over me.

"Hil just know that it's not easy talking to the ones you love about the hardships you're facing."

"I hear you shorty, but that was my blood. I should have known something was going on with her. Was I so caught up in my own world that I didn't know that my baby sister was suffering?"

The tears continued to fall, and I kept wiping them away. Once his face was dry, I sat up and placed him in my arms. His body was tense at first, but after some time, he finally relaxed and began caressing my arms. I had no clue what we were doing, but at this moment, everything felt right. He needed me, and I needed him. We might not speak about this tomorrow, but for tonight, this was all that mattered.

As I laid my head against the headboard, I wondered what my life would be like with him. I knew that a woman as broken as I was shouldn't be thinking about being with another man, but here I was. The more I thought about it, the more I wanted to run and hide. We shouldn't be here with each other like this. We needed to go back to barely talking to one another and only seeing each other in passing.

It was time for him to go. The longer he stayed here, the deeper my feelings grew. We couldn't be a thing no matter how hard we tried. I looked down at him and went to open my mouth, but the warmth of his lips quickly covered it. He placed his hand behind my head and intertwined my hair in his fingers. The feeling of his warm tongue dancing with mine caused heat to travel throughout my body. This felt so right, yet so wrong, as I released a soft moan. The kiss intensified as my tiny fingers roamed his chest and his arms. His hand found its way under my shirt and caressed my breasts. My hips began to move back and forth rhythmically. It's been a long time since a man touched me, and I felt myself getting ready to explode. I was on the brink of an orgasm, but he pulled his hand from under my shirt and pulled our lips apart. Finally, our lips separated, and we engaged in an intense staredown.

Slivers of moonlight traveled through the blinds and landed perfectly on his handsome face. He sat up in front of me in an ape-like stance and bit on his bottom lip. The sight before me was intimidating yet satisfying at the same time. I wanted nothing more than to pull him down on top of me and indulge in all the things I've been dreaming about.

"I want nothing more than to be the one to take you on that wave of ecstasy, but we aren't ready for that yet." My mouth fell open so fast that it caused pain to shoot through me.

"Kay, Rose cares a lot about you, and I'm starting to see why. You try to see the good in people and situations, and that shit is admirable, even when it's wasted on stupid ass people. I stand firm in what I said about not teaching you to shoot. However, I will teach you how to defend yourself. I'll hit you up when it's time to start your training." He placed a kiss on my forehead, got off the bed, and headed out the door.

I can't begin to describe what I was feeling. There was nothing else that I could do except try to go to sleep and forget that this ever happened.

The sun shined through the shades waking me up from a peaceful sleep. It was a beautiful Saturday summer morning, and I had a few things on my to-do list. As I showered and prepared for my day of doing nothing, my mind started wandering to Manahil. It's been a few days since we had our little moment, and I couldn't stop thinking about it. I would wake up in the middle of the night in a cold sweat from dreaming about it. My dreams were vivid and felt so real.

We continued to only see each other in passing, and not many words were said. It was honestly quite awkward. Rose has picked up on our strange encounters and has even tried to question me about it, but my lips are sealed. If he wasn't going to acknowledge what happened that night, then neither was I. Yes, I know that it's childish, but it is what it is.

As I lay on the living room couch, my mind drifted back to that night. I wished that I were more confident in myself so that I could have seized the moment. It seems like there's so much more to Hil, and I found myself wanting to know everything about him, but I don't feel that I'm the right girl for him. Dealing with a broken woman isn't something that many men tend to want in life. So, despite what my heart and body were feeling, I decided to follow my mind and just continue working on me. If I continued to dwell on this any further, then I would end up crying uncontrollably, and honestly,

I was tired of crying. The ringing of my phone snapped me out of my thoughts.

"Hey, Ladybug!" Oya screamed from the other end.

"What's up, Ya?"

"So, I was thinking that we go and have a girl's day. I have my trio clients at ten a.m., but after them, I am free for the day. My assistants will be there to help, so we should be done by one o'clock. Are you good with that? We should get our nails done, grab some lunch, and then do some shopping. I miss my best girl, and we have a lot to catch up on," she pouted in the phone.

"Yeah, that's a good time for me. I have an appointment in about thirty minutes, so I should probably get going. Call me when you're done. Love you." We said our goodbyes and got off the phone.

This was perfect timing on her part because I was planning on calling her and telling her that I was going to come to pick her up. She had been a little distant lately, and I wanted to make sure she was good. I had yet to tell her my feelings about Manahil, and I think that this would be a perfect time. Hopefully, she would help me settle the fight going on between my head and my heart.

Just as I was about to get in the shower and get my day started, my phone rang. I wasn't expecting any calls at this time. When I saw that it was a number that wasn't saved, uncertainty and uneasiness rang through my body. Lately, I've been receiving phone calls from unknown numbers, but no one ever said anything. At this point, I was fed the fuck up.

"Hello?" I waited and waited, but they didn't say anything. "Stop fuckin' playing on my phone. If you have something you want to stay, then I suggest you say it. If not, stop fuckin' calling me!"

I wish I still had a flip phone so that I could slam it shut! Pressing the end button didn't give off the same attitude. Hopefully, whoever it was got the picture and would stop calling.

CHAPTER FOURTEEN
OYA ZAIRE

THE LAST FEW days were nothing shy of a hot ass mess. Mase and I weren't on speaking terms whatsoever, but the fact of the matter is, he had yet to reach out to me. I know that I wasn't talking to him, but I would have felt so much better if he had called. I'm sure that he was somewhere with Mya, but if he didn't produce himself soon, then shit was going to get ugly in the city of Chicago. One thing I don't allow is for a nigga to fuck with my heart, and Mase was currently foot working on it.

In order for me not to think about my issues with Mase, I decided that having a girl's day with Kay would be the best thing to do. It would take my mind off the situation, and I would get dolled up in the process. It was a win-win situation if you ask me. I also needed to speak to Kay about the whole Nix situation. Every day since the night he dropped me off, he made sure to call or text me. I knew that two wrongs don't make a right, but if Mase was out here having his fun why couldn't I.

I needed to get it together because my head was all over the place as I readied my station. The bell to the shop dinged, and my first client was right on time. These clients were high profile, so I didn't mind shutting down the shop for them.

"Blair! How are you?"

"Oya, I'm good. How are you?"

Her girls Rhyland and Abri walked in behind her, and we continued the small talk. It felt good to be around a group of women that were about their business. Just like in any other shop, we talk, laugh, and cry. Today was no different.

"Okay, so what are you getting today? Deep condition and curly?" Blair was a pretty simple girl when it came to her looks. She always got a deep condition and kept it curly whenever she came to see me.

"Nah, not this time. Can you flat iron and trim me?"

I was honestly shocked. B had rarely switched things up when it came to her hair. That is except the time she cut it off after she went missing in action for a few weeks. The girl had the whole city looking for her. Read all about that in *Perfect Dreams & Hood Nightmares: A Deadly Love Affair*. I was heated when she sashayed her ass in this shop showing off her handy work. She didn't do a bad job, but baby girl had inches for days and put a bunch of these bald headed chicks to shame.

"Well okay then, Mrs. Bellevue, whatever you like." She laughed and waved me off. I escorted her to the shampoo bowl, and we got right to it. As I was shampooing her hair, my mind drifted to Mase.

"What's on your mind, O? I've been talking for five minutes, and you have yet to say a word? Talk to me," B asked, snapping me out of my thoughts.

I didn't want to talk about it, but I knew that I needed to get it off my chest. Once I gave her a full rundown, the whole shop was quiet. No one wanted to be the first to say anything, and I could understand why. You have to be cautious when it comes to other people's relationships and emotions. Not everyone is equipped for the honest to God truth.

"He's still breathing?" Rhyland broke the silence, and everyone erupted into laughter.

"Yeah girl, for now." The look on her face had me cracking up.

"Nah ma, she's dead ass serious," B said while shaking her head. "You know Rhy; she's a special kinda crazy. Don't pay her any attention, but I want to hear what you feel you should do before I shoot you my answer."

"I need to assess the situation before I move further. In my younger days, I would have shot that damn restaurant up and asked questions later, but God has been working on me. I really need to know who the fuck she is. That's what's bothering me the most."

"What's the bitch—I mean, what's the broad's info?" Rhy spoke up while pulling her phone out.

"Um, all I know is that her name is Mya and she worked at Capital Grille. I know that's not helpful, but shit that's all I—"

"Cool." She held up her finger to place me on hold.

"You're the best, baby," she cooed into the phone.

"Now that we have her information, what do you plan on doing with it? I've been at home with my daughter for a minute, and I'm all for coming out of retirement," Abri stated while getting up from the chair and putting her hair into a ponytail.

"Sit down Wreck-It Ralph!" B yelled out. "It's broad ass daylight, and you don't even know if she wants to run up on the broad or not. You are turned up lately. You good, ma?"

"Yeah, I'm good, B. You know I just don't tolerate no bullshit. Plain and simple," she shrugged and let my assistant finish her hair.

Rhy let me know that her man Que had a whole file on Mya, and he would send it over to my house that night through one of his buddies. I appreciated the connections that they had because lord knows it would have taken me a hell of a lot longer to find out what I needed without them. I let Abri know that I would handle this on my own, but I would definitely call her if I needed any assistance.

An hour later we were finished, and I was in tears dealing with these three. It was always fun having the girls in the shop. We kissed each other goodbye and scheduled their next appointments.

As I cleaned up the shop, I decided to give Kay a call. I was a little excited to be spending time with the bestie. I missed her something serious. It's been tough on the both of us not being close to each other as we've been used to. I also figured that she would want to hear about the whole Mase and Mya situation.

"Hey, Kay."

"Hey Ya, you ready for today? Where you wanna meet?" She sounded so bubbly and full of excitement that it made my heart smile.

"If you want you can meet me at the lofts, and we can jump in one car. It'll be easier that way. Is that cool with you?" The silence from the other end of the phone caused me to look at the screen to see if I had lost the connection. "Kay, mama, you there?"

"Y-yes, um okay. I'll see you there. Love you, bye."

The call disconnected, and I knew that something else was going on with Kay and I needed to find out why, quickly. But before I could grab my things and head out the door, the sound of bass bumping down the street let me know that my day was about to get worse before it got better. I quickly locked the doors of the shop and cut off all the lights. I needed for it to appear as if I wasn't there.

Unfortunately, he knew better, and I should have known better too. Mase helped design my shop and funded nearly eighty percent of the renovation costs. Of course, this man had a key. I have got to do better when it comes to thinking quickly. There was only one door in this whole shop that he didn't have a key to and that was my supply closet. I had a lock installed after the renovations were complete, so there was no need to give him a key. As quietly as I could, I snuck into the supply closet and locked the door.

"Oya, I know you're in there. Please come out and just talk to me. Let me explain." I thought I was ready to hear an explanation from him, but now that the opportunity presented itself, I didn't want to hear it.

"Just go away. Whatever you and that woman have going on is none of my business."

Tears had formed in my eyes, and I couldn't stop them from coming down. I had serious trust issues when it came to men due to previous relationships, but when Mase came around, he swept me off my feet and changed all of that.

"Order's up!" Hal called out from the kitchen window. "Hey Oya, how are you today? I haven't seen you in a while."

"I'm doing good Hal, just working like crazy. You know I graduate in a few weeks, right?"

"Wow." He wiped his hands off on his apron and came around to the front of the diner.

I was currently in one of my favorite diner's grabbing a bite to eat after a long day at the shop. My hard work was going to pay off one day. One of these days I'm going to own my own shop and sell my very own products. Nevertheless, until that day comes, I'll continue giving booth rent to Celest and working my ass off to get this degree.

"Oya, you've been coming to this diner for years, and I can't begin to explain to you, how proud you've made me. Despite everything you've been through, you've continued to push and make the best out of a horrible situation."

I tried my best to not think about what I've gone through to get here, but it was hard. Losing both my parents at an early age took a toll on me, physically and emotionally. No one thinks that their life would change in an instant at such an early age, but that was my reality, many, many years ago.

"Aye Hal, sup big homie?" A male voice snapped me out of my dark place and brought me back to reality.

"Mayson, I haven't seen you in ages. I guess this is surprise an old man day, two of my favorite youngins both here at the same time."

Hal came from behind the counter and hugged him while handing him a white envelope. It wasn't any of my business, but I'm almost certain that it contained money. I've been around the block a few times and knew how all of worked.

"Oya, I would like for you to meet my nephew."

"H-hey," was all I managed to get out as he reached his hand out for me to shake. I put mine in his, and a perfect smile formed on his face.

"Hey to you too."

Our eyes remained on one another until a young woman came and interrupted us. She was gorgeous with her curly blonde hair, emerald green eyes, and shapely body. No one in here could deny her beauty.

"Monsieur, I thought you said you'd be in and out. Come on. We have some shopping to do," she said as she placed her arm around his. She smiled at me and stuck out her hand for me to shake. "Hi, I'm Mya. Have you two met before?"

"Nope, we just met today. Nice talking to all of you. Hal, I'm gone. I'll see you soon," I explained without shaking her hand.

I grabbed my things, placed my money on the counter, and started walking out of the door. Hal tried calling me back, but I didn't have the time.

That flashback had ignited a fire within me. I had met Mya before, and it completely escaped my mind. After that encounter, I hadn't seen Mase around the diner until a few months later. During that time, he pursued me hard, and a friendship started. Then it grew into a full-blown relationship. He assured me that Mya was a distant memory and that I wouldn't have to worry about her a day in my life.

Unlocking the supply closet, I saw that he was sitting in a chair with his head in his hands. I reached over into one of the stations and grabbed a pair of sheers. He had some explaining to do, and I needed answers right this second. He wasn't going to get away with doing me dirty.

"You got two minutes to plead your case before I have you bleeding on my marble floor," I spoke through gritted teeth while holding the sheers to his neck.

"Woah, this how you comin,' Ya? You threatening my life?"

"Hell yeah, I told you not to fuck with me because I'm not all the way right in the head. I've killed once, and I'll damn sure do it again."

The words flowed effortlessly out of my mouth, and I didn't mean for that to come out, but the secret was out, and there's no turning back.

"W-what? What did you just say? Ya, you out here catchin' bodies and failed to tell me that shit?"

"This ain't about what I did in my past. This is about you and Mya. I remember meeting her the same day that we met for the first time at Hal's. She broke your fuckin' heart Mase, and I put that shit back together again. You really let me leave that restaurant without coming to get me. It's obvious that you aren't over her!"

He tried to grab my hand that held the sheers, but I backed away from him. I don't know who I had just become, but this wasn't me. Loving this man was turning me into a complete idiot. I had a life to live and a business to run, and I refuse to mess that up over someone who didn't give a damn about me.

"It's time for you to leave, Mase," I said while throwing the sheers on the countertop.

"Oya, please just let me explain. I know it sounds crazy but please just let me explain," he pleaded, but I wasn't interested in anything he had to say. Maybe one day I'll sit down with him and let him talk, for closure purposes, but right now, I needed him out of my space before I did something I regret.

"Goodbye Mase," I pointed towards the door and thankfully, he left without a fight. I'm sure this wasn't the last that we would see of each other.

CHAPTER FIFTEEN
KARMA WHITE

RETURNING to the lofts wasn't something that I was ready for right now. The scars from Zo were finally healing, but they were still visible. Honestly, I think it might be time for me to give that apartment up. It held too many bad memories, and I need to move on with my life. Zo would be dealt with in a timely manner, but I wasn't physically and mentally ready yet.

Pushing past the hurt and pain, I drove towards the lofts. I pulled into the parking lot next to Oya's car and shut the car off. She was sitting in her car texting away on her phone. It seems as though something was troubling her. I stepped out of my car and went to knock on her window. She jumped in her seat and dropped the phone on the floor.

"Don't scare me like that!" she yelled with her hand over her chest.

"Pop the locks, and let's go get some food." She smiled at the mention of food.

We arrived at a place that we had been dying to try, and now that I had my wires out, I was going to enjoy this even more. We were seated immediately, and we buried our heads into the menus to figure out what we were going to try first. The waitress had come by and taken our orders, and then an awkward silence fell over us. It was as if we both wanted to spill out information, but no one wanted to go first.

"I don't want you to be mad, but I need to tell you what happened the other day," I took a sip of my Moscow Mule and waited for her reaction. She leaned back in her chair and folded her arms. I hated bringing this news to Oya, and I'm sure she was tired of all things Karma and Lorenzo.

"The day that I left your shop, I went back to the loft to get my editing bin. As you know, I'm still trying to keep my business afloat and keep the money rolling in. That bin has everything that I need, and there's no way that I can do what I do without it."

She raised her eyebrow and continued to listen.

"While I was there, I had an unwanted visitor—"

"Wait you mean like a rat or something? What you mean unwanted?" I now had her full attention, and if I didn't say something soon, things were going to go bad.

"No, not like a rat, Oya. Lorenzo came busting in the door. We had a minor altercation, but the damage was minimal. He didn't get the best of me this time. We fought, and I stabbed him in the arm with the elephant that was on my coffee table."

"Did you kill him?" she leaned over and whispered to me.

"No, I didn't kill him Ya, at least not this time."

"You should have killed him," she said with disappointment in her voice.

I continued explaining to Oya what happened that night. I was giving her a full play by play, and she was eating it up like it was a movie playing on the big screen. When I was done, she just grabbed her glass of wine and chugged the whole thing.

"Wow, I have no words right now."

She flagged down the waiter to get her another glass of wine.

"Well, ma'am, I guess it's time for me to tell you what I've been going through," she said while taking a deep breath.

When she finished explaining to me everything that took place between her and Mase, I was ready to find him. This was all too much, and something needed to shake. On the bright side, I was more interested to know about this Nix character. She may not have known it, but she was blushing when she spoke on him.

"It's okay, Kay. I know it's a lot to take in. My mind is every-where, but I'm gonna be good. I promise."

"I know you're going to be good. That's not what I'm afraid of. I'm afraid of you taking out all of your frustrations on this new guy. Yeah, I'm going to need more info on that."

"Yeah, there's really not more information to give. He wants it to be more, but I'm not ready for that right now."

I don't know who she was fooling, but there was definitely a part of her that wanted more with this new guy, but the other part of her is still caught up on Mase, and the new guy doesn't deserve only half of her.

Once we finished dinner, we decided to head back to Rose's house and chill out like old times. We needed to be there for each other, and what better way to do that than wine and popcorn. After our store run, we made it to the house, and I noticed a car in the driveway that didn't belong. Oya noticed it too, and her whole vibe changed.

"Come on, don't worry about who's in here. Let's just head straight to my room."

"Maybe we should just go to my house," Oya said while putting her seatbelt back on.

"No, we're going to bypass him and whoever he's brought in here. My room is in a completely different section of the house. They'll barely even see us. Now come on. We have wine, popcorn, and food to enjoy."

"Okay, I'm liking bossy Kay. Keep that up." She snapped her fingers, and we got out the car.

As we walked towards the house, my mind started to go to a dark place. I wanted to know who he had in the house, but then again it was none of my business.

When we walked past the living room where he was, a wave of relief came over me. Thankfully, he wasn't in there with a woman. I didn't think he'd be that disrespectful, but then again, I didn't put much past him. He and another man were camped out playing a video game. Snacks and drinks covered the coffee table, and if Rose were here, she would have a fit. He knew better than to be in her front room making a mess.

"You better clean that up before Rose sees and beats ya ass," I mumbled as we walked past.

The gentleman he was with turned around and laughed, but his smile quickly faded when he saw Oya. She was typing away on her phone, so she didn't realize that she was being watched.

"Ahem, ahem," I nudged her, and her head shot up. Their eyes connected, and she took off running towards the back of the house.

"Someone wanna tell me what the hell just happened?" Manahil asked. He was just as confused as I was.

"You know her, fam?" he asked his friend. He shook his head tried to follow her, but I stopped him. "I don't know you like that, so I'm gonna need you to stay right here. Let me go talk to her first." I looked him up and down, and he held his hands up in surrender.

CHAPTER SIXTEEN
OYA ZAIRE

I HADN'T SEEN Nix since the night he was my Uber driver. We still talked every single day, but I wasn't ready to face him just yet. I didn't mean to run off, but the butterflies that formed in my stomach scared the hell out of me.

"Oya! Where are you?" Karma yelled from down the hall. She was going to find me eventually, so I decided against saying anything. I just opened the bottle of wine and started drinking straight from it.

"Woah lil mama, I'm not sure what's going on with you but guzzling a bottle of wine is not the answer." Kay came and snatched the bottle of wine from me.

"Hey, give that back!" I reached for the bottle, but she held it far away from me.

"No, not until you explain to me what the hell is going on. Who is that man, and why does he have you running away from him? Wait is that *him?*"

Kay sat down on the floor next to me and poured me a glass of wine. My lack of response gave everything away.

"Oh shit, this is the kind of excitement that I need in my life. Why are you running from him?"

"The butterflies started, and I wasn't ready for it. I just had this whole thing with Mase, and I don't want to deal with him today too. I'm exhausted, Kay, mentally exhausted."

I chugged the glass of wine and waited for her to say something.

"Well, I hate to be the bearer of bad news, but you're going to have to deal with him today whether you like it or not. You know he's gonna make it this way now that he knows y'all are in the same place. It's inevitable. At least he's cute," she said with a wink.

No sooner than the words left her mouth someone knocked on the door. She went to answer the door, but I pulled her back down.

"Don't open that door," I plead, but it fell on deaf ears. Kay snatched away from me and opened it. She waved goodbye to me and left me to deal with this on my own.

On the other side of the door, Nix stood there with one of his hands in his pocket and the other behind his back, allowing me the chance to take all of him in. He was handsome, but that's not what attracted me to him. He kept things light and simple. There wasn't a flashy bone in his body. His clothes were simple, and his jewelry was almost non-existent. Dressed in black from his shirt to his shoes, he was a sight to see.

"That boyfriend of yours still ain't acting right?" he said and just like that, I wanted to lay hands on him.

"Nix, we're not about to have this conversation. You can see your way out of here and let my friend know that she can come back."

"Nah, I saw that my Lois Lane needed savin', so that's what I'm here to do." He licked his lips and flashed that smile at me.

"Wait, how do you know Manahil?"

I wasn't going to acknowledge the other stuff he had to say. Mase and I were in a horrible place, but that doesn't mean that I'm supposed to let another man come in and take my mind off that. We had some shit to figure out. Either we were going to be together, or we weren't.

"We work together."

"Manahil works for Uber too? Nah, he can't work for Uber

affording houses like this. Now, I'm gonna ask again, and I would like the truth. Where you know him from?"

"You ask a lot of questions that you don't need the answer to. Who said anything about only having *one* job? Just know I'm a friend, and we work together. Let's switch gears though. How's the boyfriend? Have y'all reconciled?" He leaned against the doorpost and looked at me like he was actually interested in what I had to say. We both know that he was fishing for information about my relationship status.

"Now who's asking too many questions?" He let out a low chuckle and shook his head.

"I'm glad I was finally able to catch up with you. You're hard to track down. I'd given up hope that I'd see you today. I guess this is fate. A friend of mine told me to give you this." He walked towards me and handed me a manila folder.

It took me a minute to realize what was in my hand. Earlier at the shop, Rhyland's boyfriend let me know that someone would be dropping off information to me about Mya.

When he placed the folder in my hand, it felt like a ton of bricks. The fate of the world as I knew it relied on what was in this folder. I didn't know whether to open it or throw it out the window. After much deliberation, I finally opened it and flipped through as much as I could before I ran to the bathroom and emptied the contents of my stomach. The folder was filled with old and new photos of Mase and Mya. I don't know what kind of sick shit they were into, but we damn sure didn't do any of this.

"Oya, you good?" Nix asked while searching for a towel. He knew I wasn't okay. He knew what was in that folder and didn't even give me a fair warning. I just shook my head and hugged the toilet. This was all too much for me to deal with.

"Here, let me help you." I turned to face him, and he began cleaning my mouth with a warm rag. "You ready for me to save you yet?"

He had just ruined a perfectly good setup. The fact that he cared enough to come to help me was softening my heart, unfortunately, that Superman and Lois Lane shit was working my nerves. I snatched the rag away from him while making sure to roll my eyes and finished wiping my mouth.

"Why are you ignoring the chemistry between us?"

He stood up and helped me off up the floor. We were now standing with only a few inches between us. He licked his lips, and I found myself wanted to be his tongue. The lump in my throat caused me to take a few steps back and regain focus.

"I'm not ignoring the chemistry between us. It's just we can't do *this*. This thing between us can't move forward. Even though Mase and I are done, I'm not ready to jump into anything else," I stated.

I began searching in the cabinets for a spare toothbrush. I needed to get this taste out of my mouth, and it wasn't fair to Nix for me to be in his face with foul breath. Thankfully, I found a brand new one under the sink along with toothpaste. As I brushed away the vomit, Nix looked at me with uncertainty written all over his face. When I finished brushing my teeth, I moved past him, walked back into the room, and plopped down on the bed.

"You sure you don't want *this*?"

He walked over to me and ran the tips of his fingers up my arm, causing my body to shutter. He dipped his head into the crook of my neck and blew soft, warm air. The tingling caused my eyes to shut, and a soft moan escaped out my mouth. His hands continued to travel up and down my arms, and then they found their way to the nape of my neck. My neck was the most sensitive part of my body, and with one simple touch, a storm would form within me. It was just my luck when Nix found it and softly caressed it. I needed to get away from him, but my body wasn't on the same page as my brain. I could only take so much of this torture.

"Ss-stop. Please, stop, we can't. We can't do this," I cried out in ecstasy.

"Do you really want me to stop, Oya?"

In my mind, I was screaming out *yes,* but I shook my head no. He stood me up, turned me around, and placed his arms around me. The feeling of being in his arms was something new to me— protection. I felt like I was safe and secure.

CHAPTER SEVENTEEN
KARMA WHITE

OYA COULD DENY her feelings for Nix all she wanted to, but I knew better. He had her flustered, and it was actually funny to see. Initially, I had let them have their privacy, but when I heard the door close, curiosity got the best of me, and I needed to know what was happening. I pressed my ear against the door, and my face turned bright red. Soft moans were coming from Oya's mouth. *Okay Nix, I see you!* As long as he treats my girl right, then I'm all for this.

"Come on, nosey ass girl. Give them some privacy," Hil whispered in my ear, causing me to jump. I forgot that he had followed me here. "I'm sure she'll explain everything when the time is right. For now, just give her some space to figure out what's going on."

"How do you know him?" I asked as Hil dragged me back to the living room.

"Nix and I go way back. We're in the same line of work. He's good peoples, so she's in good hands."

"Did you know about this?"

"Nah," he said without looking at me. He was lying, but I wasn't going to push the subject.

Not wanting to focus on this any longer I pulled out my phone and started searching the web. If I didn't divert my attention away from Manahil, then I would do something I regret.

"What's your favorite color?"

As soon as it came out of my mouth, I knew just how corny it sounded. That's typically not the first question you ask a man that you're trying to get to know. I wanted to run and hide but the damage was done, and I needed to handle this. A chuckle escaped his lips, and I realized that was the first time I had ever heard him laugh.

"Black, how about you?" Wow, I was so taken aback that I forgot to answer his question. He had actually answered it and did it without being a smart ass.

"You gonna tell me yours or not?"

"S-sorry, it's turquoise."

"Yeah, shorty, you're different. Why can't you have a normal favorite color like pink or purple? Why do you have to like complicated shit like that?" He was now in a fit of laughter.

"I don't know. I've loved it since I was a little girl. Hell, you wanna talk about me? Why is your favorite color black?" He just shrugged his shoulders and continued to play the game.

The wine had me feeling myself just a little bit, so I snatched the controller out of his hand and began playing the game for him.

"Kay, give me the controller back before you fuck up my game." He reached over and tried to grab it, but I paused the game and stretched my arm as far as I could. "You really wanna play with me? Is that really what you want to do?"

"You aren't going to do anything. Sit back and watch me play the game."

I pushed him back and un-paused the game. Hil probably thought that I didn't know what I was doing. I learned to play during the many days that I spent in the house while with Zo. Sometimes the beatings were so severe that I'd be in the house for days while the bruises healed. I continued to play the game and tried to not go into my dark place.

"Give me the damn controller before you make me lose this game."

He pulled me into his arms, and I found myself straddling him. We sat like this for a few minutes, neither of us wanting to make the next move. His chocolate skin framed his dark eyes perfectly. He swiped his pink tongue against his lips, and I couldn't help myself. I needed to taste those lips again. It has been far too long since they were up against mine. I thought that he would stop me, but he happily accepted my advances.

This kiss had me on cloud one hundred and ninety-nine. I didn't want it to end, but I felt his nature rising, and his hands found their way under my shirt. He was right. I wasn't ready for that yet, especially not on Rose's couch. Reluctantly, I pulled away.

"You aren't ready, and that's cool," he said as I climbed off him. He took the controller and continued to play the game. The silence was awkward, and I needed to fix that.

"When can we start my training?"

"Be ready tomorrow at five a.m.," he said without taking his eyes off the TV.

Looking at the clock on the wall, I noticed that it was going on ten p.m. If I was going to be ready for this training, then I needed to get some sleep. Unfortunately, my room was still occupied. I grabbed a throw blanket out of the linen closet, snuggled up on the couch opposite of Manahil, and drifted off to sleep.

The feeling of fingers in my hair caused me to stir out of my sleep. It felt so good that I didn't want it to stop. Whoever was playing in my hair was gentle yet masculine. They kept massaging my scalp, causing me to moan out in pleasure. Before I knew it, I was being picked up and carried somewhere. When I opened my eyes, Hil had picked me up bridal style. I don't know what prompted him to do this, but I didn't want it to end. Nothing in my life felt better than this moment right here.

"Where are you taking me? Is Oya still here?"

"Yeah, she's still here," he said, but he didn't answer where he was taking me. I was too sleepy to fight him. I'd just find out when we got there.

"You know I can walk right?" I said with a small giggle.

"Yeah, I do. Do you want me to put you down?" I quickly shook my head no.

"I didn't think so," he said while gently laying me on the bed.

He went to place the blanket over me, and I caught a whiff of it. It finally dawned on me that I was in the room that he stays in when he's here. The fact that he felt comfortable enough to bring me in his space was enough to make me smile. He was warming up to me, and maybe it was time for me to let my guard down. Hil keeps telling me that I'm not ready for him, but in all actuality, he wasn't ready for me. Once I start, there's no turning me off, and I wasn't sure how he was going to react to that.

He laid the cover near my chin, and I grabbed his arm and pulled him down towards me. He ended up losing his balance and fell on top of me. It was silly, and we shared in a laugh.

"Is this your way of taking charge?" He asked with a raised eyebrow, and in return, I licked my lips and pulled him down. Our lips touched, and my body shuttered underneath him.

"Are you sure you want to do this?" he questioned.

"I'm ready," I confidently stated as I pushed the blanket off me.

I pulled my shirt over my head and exposed the upper part of my body. He was wearing a simple white shirt and gray jogging pants. I pulled on his shirt and guided it up his body and over his arms. It was now or never.

His chest and abs were staring me in my face, and they were sculpted to perfection. I began placing soft kisses on them and his body shuttered. When I looked up at him, he had his eyes closed while biting on his bottom lip. Manahil wasn't used to a woman taking care with him, but I was about to change that. Before he knew it, I had turned him over on his back and straddled him. A scowl graced his face, but it'll change by the time I'm done with him.

"Are you ready for this?"

"Kay gets a little confidence in her and wants to hang with a big boy. I like this look—" He tried to keep talking, but I was done. We needed this to happen for a number of reasons.

I covered his mouth with mine and kissed him passionately. His hands found their way to my back, and I deepened our kiss. From the way he was holding me, I knew that this was more than just sex. This was love, but neither one of us wanted to say anything. We were too afraid of what the other person would think.

It was time. It was time to explore his body, and there was no turning back. I needed to know what makes his body shake, what makes him cum, is he a pleaser, or is he a taker. I wanted to know it all.

I began placing soft kisses down from his chest down to his stomach. When I reached the top of his sweats, I used my teeth and moved them away from his skin. This little trick made him cock his head to the side in surprise. A smirk crossed my face as I pulled out his throbbing nature. He didn't know what I was going to do with it, but he was down for the ride.

When it pulled it out of his boxers, it stood straight up, ready for me to devour it. He was a nice decent size, and I could get with this. It wasn't too big, but it wasn't small. It's like it was perfect to me. My mouth salivated at the sight of it. Before he could protest, I placed it in my mouth and began sucking slowly but making sure to keep my mouth tight. His body moved under me, and I knew that I had him right where I wanted him. As I sucked, I removed my pants and mentally prepared myself for what was about to take place.

CHAPTER EIGHTEEN
MANAHIL REEVES

I DIDN'T EXPECT things between Kay and me to go there, but it did, and I don't regret it. It shocked the shit out of me that she took charge. She knew she wasn't ready before, and I'm glad she finally found her confidence.

We were lying in bed, and she was sleeping peacefully under my arm. My mind was running a thousand miles a minute as I thought about what we could be. I told myself a long time ago that love wasn't for me. I've seen firsthand what it can do to a person, but when I'm around Karma, I find it harder and harder to run from it. She's a special woman, and the sooner she realizes it, the sooner she's going to be a force to be reckoned with. Damn, Rose was right. Baby girl is definitely a Phoenix.

My phone started ringing, and my mood immediately shifted. It had to be a job, and that meant I had to get out the bed. I've never thought about retiring from my line of work until right now.

"Yeah."

"Young Hil, how are you?" Hassim asked from the other end. Two calls in less than a month were starting to make me suspicious.

"I was sleeping peacefully. What's up though, I'm almost positive you don't give a damn about how I'm doing or how I'm sleepin'. What's really the purpose of this call?"

"Meet me outside in twenty minutes," he demanded and hung up.

Heat radiated off of my body, and Kay started to stir in her sleep. Hassim was gettin' comfortable with callin' my phone on bullshit. We didn't need to talk about shit that didn't involve work. If he was gonna ask me about Kay, then he better be prepared for my reaction.

Twenty minutes later, headlights were pulling into the driveway. Sim put his car in park and stepped out like he was about to do a photo shoot for GQ, despite the fact that it was 2:30 in the morning. He approached me, and we shook hands.

"We need to have a conversation. Do you know who Karma White really is?" I had a feeling that shit was about to get more real than I wanted them to. "Get in, let's go for a ride."

"Let's go, Kay! You better not give up. You gotta fight, ma. Push through it," I yelled at Karma as if her life depended on it. "We're almost done. You got this shit!"

Today was Kay's first day of training with me. Her body was in good shape, so the physical activity wasn't difficult for her. That would change soon. I was going to push her harder than she's ever been pushed before. There had been plenty of times during this one day where she wanted to give up, but she didn't fold. She ended up shocking the shit out of me.

"Ahhh!!" she yelled at she reached the top of the hill. We had completed a three-mile run and shorty was exhausted and damn near about to fall out. She was so proud of herself for completing it, but I had to be the bearer of bad news.

"You know we have to go back, right? That'll be a total of six miles. You ready for that or do I need to call an Uber."

Her eyes looked as if they were going to pop out of her damn head when she heard that. As she tried to steady her breathing, a black Audi rolled past us slowly. It was Hassim, and I needed for him to chill out. Kay wasn't paying attention to it, but I was. If she was going to fuck with me, then she needed to be aware of her surrounding like her life depended on it. Little did she know, it did.

"Oh, you've got to be out of your rabid ass mind. Really Hil? You couldn't have said that *before* we started running. I would have done one mile there and one mile back. My mind nor my body is prepared to go back. You've—"

"Calm down, shorty. You got this. You've done great for it to be your first day. I think it's because you have the best teacher there is." I flashed a smile at her and in return, she stuck up her middle finger and started running back.

"Tell me what's the deal with you. You keep asking me questions about my past, but you've never touched bases on yours. You're like a mystery to me."

"Well, my childhood was kind of depressing. I'll tell you, but only if you feel like hearing a sob story."

"Man, come on with it. Your shit can't be any worse than mine."

"Okay don't say I didn't warn you." She shrugged her shoulders and continued running. "Where should I start. Let's start at my conception. From what I've been told, my mother was in a relationship with a married man. All her life she was screaming up and down how she wasn't going to get pregnant and them boom, she got pregnant with me. No one had ever come right out and told me the meaning behind my name. But from what I've gathered, it came from me being my mother's karma for messing with him."

She was dropping bricks on me, and I had nothing to say. She continued talking about her childhood, and it was some of the most heart-wrenching shit I've ever heard. Karma has been through some things, and you would never know it. She didn't wear her struggles, and I admired that about her.

"I've practically raised myself. My mother is still alive, but we haven't spoken in years. It's better this way. I graduated from high school and college on time. Oh, I'm debt free as well. No student loans formed against me shall prosper. I plan on going back to get my masters one of these days, but only when I'm good and damn ready."

"Wow, that's what's up. You said you don't know who your dad is right. Have you ever tried to find out who he was?"

"Yeah, I've tried to ask my mom a few times, but she would always change the subject. One time she slipped up and told me his name was Hassim. That'll be like a needle in a haystack to find. But I'm good! I'm turning my life around, and I'm finally getting back to me. I don't want to dwell on my sad ass childhood anymore."

The conversation that I had with Hassim the other day was starting to make sense. I found it unusual that he wanted to know as much about Kay and her past as he could. This nigga was her daddy, and he knew it. He was using me to find out more information about her. It took everything in me not to tell her everything I knew, but at the end of the day it wasn't my place, and I didn't want to crush her spirit. When the time comes, she will have answers to all the questions that she's been having since she was little.

CHAPTER NINETEEN
LORENZO LAMONT

I'D BEEN CAMPED out at my homegirl Juelz house since my first encounter with Karma. The shit was bothering me in more ways than one. I wasn't sure if she had gone to the police, and I damn sure wasn't trying to find out. Laying low was my best option until I found out what was really going on, especially after the incident at her apartment that left me with a stab wound to the shoulder. There was something about this relationship that I just couldn't shake. Karma is my soulmate, and I refuse to let anyone tell me otherwise. We're in a rough patch right now, but we were going to be together again and living our best lives.

Currently, I was laid out on Juelz's couch after taking a few Percs to get my mind off of my shitty ass situation, and the pain in my shoulder. I lacked all motivation to get up and do my day-to-day stuff, and things weren't looking good for my dealerships. Usually, Kay would be there to push me and keep me going, but without her, I realize that I am nothing. She knew when I was about to slip off the deep end and would grab me before I was too far gone.

"Thank you for taking care of everything, Nikki. Mr. Lamont is feeling better and will be back in the office soon. Continue to keep the business running per usual. Have a great day," Juelz said as she hung up the phone.

I had no clue what she was doing, but the shit had me hot.

"What do you think you're doing?" I yelled as I tried to sit up from the couch. My head was spinning, and it felt like two midgets were playing full-court basketball.

"You've missed too much time at work, Zo. Your employees are calling to see if you died and they weren't informed, so I took the liberty of doing some work for you so that you can continue making money. You're welcome," Juelz said as she walked out of the room.

Just hearing her talk about my businesses caused my head to hurt even more. Juelz was the complete opposite of Karma, from their looks to their attitudes. Don't get me wrong, Juelz is a good girl and has a banging ass body, but she didn't have much else going for herself. Karma, on the other hand, had passion, drive, and wanted more out of life than to just live off a nigga's earnings.

She thought that I was battling depression along with bipolar disorder and in all honesty, she was absolutely right. I've known about my diagnosis since I was sixteen years old, and I've managed it with prescription drugs.

Six months after I got with Kay, I stopped taking them because I was better than I had ever been. I was happier, my money was looking good, and we were in a great place in our lives. We were talking about investments in our future, marriage, and kids. After that, it was murder she wrote. My attitude went from sugar to shit if the wind blew too hard. I tried to control it, but it was just too strong. Kay was aware of my constant mood swings and changes, but she never left. She only tried to help.

The more I thought about the things that Kay used to do, the more I needed her. I couldn't get better without her. Hell, I didn't want to get better without her. You never know what you have until it's gone. Against my better judgment, I called her phone.

"Hey, sorry that you missed me! Leave me a message, and I'll get back to you!"

Hearing her voice has me stuck. Memories of us came flooding back to me, and I wanted nothing more than to have her back in my grasp. She was what made me better. The phone beeped, and it was time for me to leave the message.

"Kay, it's me. I miss you, call me back." I hung up but called right back. I had more to say.

"Kay, I can't live my life without you. Baby, I'm sorry. We can make this work. I promise you that I'm sorry and I'll get help. Just come back home. Call me."

I pressed the end button and sat back on the couch. My mind wandered to what she was doing. Just hearing her sound cheerful on her voicemail caused me to think that she was out here happy, while I'm down and out. Who the hell was making her happy? What if she was with another man? I called her back and again it went to voicemail.

"Kay, why you sendin' me straight to voicemail? You got my shit blocked? When I see you I'mma fuck you up! You better not be out here with another nigga all happy and shit. I'm coming for you, Karma Jonet White. We're in this shit together forever!" I yelled into the phone and threw it against the wall, making it shatter into hundreds of pieces. "Fuck!"

"What the hell?" Juelz said as she ran back into the room. "What the hell is wrong with you, Lorenzo? Have you lost your mind?"

"I need to get Karma back." My baby was out here with another man, and I needed her back. I wasn't right without her.

"Lorenzo, sit down. You are in no shape to go anywhere. You're high and drunk as hell. Plus, your shoulder isn't fully healed yet. That's not a good combination. You need some food in your system," she said while pushing me back down on the couch. Against my better judgment, I laid back down while she switched off to the kitchen.

"Here," Juelz stood in front of me with a plate of food. Her attitude had changed, and it was evident that we were about to have some problems.

"Damn, is that all you know how to cook?"

The plate held a meal that consisted of Chicken Alfredo and store-bought garlic bread. The meal was basic and didn't require much skill. She even tried to add parsley to it to give it a better appearance. Shit, at least Karma could throw down in the damn kitchen. With her, every night was something different. That's why she was going to be the woman I spent the rest of my life with. I just had to get my shit right first.

"The good meals are for deserving ass niggas. You don't deserve nice shit with your funky ass attitude. You fail to realize that I've been here for you since day one and you're completely disregarding me for her. Newsflash, SHE LEFT YOU!"

She tried to walk off, but I grabbed her arm.

"Aye Juelz, let's not forget who bought you damn near everything you have. From this crib to that wig, I did that. Now I think you should be a little more appreciative of the things that I've given you. I think that constitutes me being a *deserving ass nigga*. Don't you think so too?"

Her eyes were wide as saucers, but she knew damn well not to test me. With my free hand, I pushed open her legs, slid two of my fingers in between her thighs, and moved them up and down. She was right where I wanted her to be. Juelz could play like she was on some tough shit, but I knew how to make her putty in my hands.

"Now, I'm gonna eat this shitty ass pasta, and when I'm done, you and I are gonna have a conversation. Got it?"

To make this situation even better I pulled her one of her breasts out of her shirt and flicked my tongue around her nipple. It instantly hardened, and Juelz began to moan while her body started to shake uncontrollably. When I released her breast, she didn't know if it was night or day.

"I-I gotta—I'll be right back," she stuttered as she ran up the stairs.

She wasn't going to get away with that attitude. Yeah, she was holding shit down since Karma left, but that didn't mean she could disrespect me like that. I was gonna let her cool down for a bit, but I intended on finishing what I started. I inhaled the pasta and sat on the couch waiting to attack my prey. The Percs were starting to set in, and it was only a matter of minutes before I was in bed sleep.

A few minutes had passed and her time was now up. I needed to get out all of today's frustrations, and Juelz was the perfect person to do it with. Her bedroom door was shut, but from this side, I could hear soft moans and a buzzing noise. As quietly as I could, I turned the knob and opened the door. Juelz was lying in bed with her legs wide open and a small vibrator moving in and out of her. Her eyes were closed as she bit down on her bottom lip. In no time, my nature was standing at attention and bursting at the seams of my jeans. My mouth watered at the sight of her juices saturating her bedspread.

Her body began to shake as she neared her peak. It was as if my body floated over to her, and before I knew it, my tongue was lapping up her natural nectar. I didn't want the taste to fade away. Her juices were quenching my thirst. She fought as hard as she could to get me to stop, but my hold on her thighs was no match for her.

"Wait, Zo," she started to tell me to stop, but it came out in a loud moan. Juelz knew she didn't want me to stop and truth be told I didn't plan on stopping. The way my dick was pulsating below me let me know that playtime was over.

As I placed kisses on her inner thigh, I took a condom out of my pocket and slid it on. I looked up and saw her rolling her eyes, but Juelz wasn't getting me like *that*. She'd been trying to get a baby out of me for a while, but she wasn't the woman that I wanted to bear my children. She's known since the beginning that she was a stress reliever and nothing more was going to come out of this situation. She seemed to have forgotten her place, but I was about to remind her.

With one hand around her throat, I squeezed lightly while spreading her legs with the other. I placed my shaft at her folds and slid the tip in. Her mouth formed the letter O, but she didn't make a sound. I took it out and placed it back in again even slower. I continued to do this until her juices rained down on me. She was right where I needed her to be. In an instant, I shoved all of me into her, and she gasped for air. My grip around her neck drew tighter as my thrusts got faster. She was experiencing the true definition of pleasure and pain. She clawed at my arm to get me to loosen my grip but again, she was no match for my strength. I knew her limit, and I wasn't going to harm her. I just needed to remind her that I was in control, and if she forgot again, I would be happy to remind her.

The faster I moved, the harder her breasts bounced in my face. They were begging for me to take them in my mouth, and I did just that. I traced her right mound with my tongue while using my free hand to toy with the other. Her body was having a hard time registering what was taking place. It didn't know whether to be pleased or be hurt.

When she began to shake violently under me, I knew that her body figured it out. Tears spilled out of her eyes as my seeds filled the condom. I released the hold on her neck and looked into her eyes. She gasped for air trying to regain her breathing pattern.

"Don't fuckin' play with me, Juelz. You already know what this is. You already know why I'm not dippin' in you bare. We can continue doing what we do how we've been doing it, or I can pack up and stop providing for you. The choice is yours."

She was still gasping for air and crying, but at this point, she was doing it to get a reaction out of me.

"You—you just tried to kill me," she said with deep breaths in between.

"But did you die?" She looked deep into my eyes and shook her head no. That's what I loved about her. She knew when to obey. I kissed her cheek, climbed out the bed, and went to shower.

As I showered, I thought about everything that I had put Kay through. I'd come to the realization that right now wasn't the best time for me to go after her. If I was going to get my woman back, then

I needed to get my shit together. Hopefully, she'll see that I'm a changed man, and then we could work it out.

I'm coming for her, and I'll kill anything that tries to stop me. No one was exempt. Karma, I'm coming for you baby.

CHAPTER TWENTY
KARMA WHITE

THINGS in my life weren't peaches and cream, but they were a lot better than they had been a few months ago. Working out with Manahil had my confidence back up, and I was finally getting back to who I was before Lorenzo. Well, maybe not that Karma, but a slightly strong version of her. I couldn't be too happy because my best friend was going through it. Her emotions were all over the place when it came to things between her and Mase, and her and Nix.

As a best friend, it was up to me to liven up her spirits, so I arranged for us to have a night out on the town. We deserved this night, and we were going to live it up and let loose. I had a whole day planned, and she was going to love it whether she liked it or not.

When I arrived in her apartment, everything was pitch black. Not an ounce of sunlight shined through her windows. When I clicked on the light, I was taken aback by how messy her apartment was. Oya is not a messy person, so this was a complete shock to me. Takeout food boxes covered her kitchen counter, and empty ice cream boxes sat sideways on her living room coffee table. I didn't plan on cleaning today, but I wasn't going to sit here with her house looking like this.

I threw my shoes by the door and started on the mess. Dishes were piled up, laundry was undone, and trash was everywhere. It's like she finished eating something and then threw it on the floor. She didn't even bother throwing it in the garbage can that was two feet away.

An hour later, I was done, and Oya had yet to emerge from her room. I didn't know what was behind that door, but I really didn't care. I wasn't cleaning up that damn mess. When I pushed open the door, it wasn't as bad as I thought it would be. There were definitely clothes everywhere, but it seems as though she kept the food outside of here.

Oya was curled up in the bed with the blanket over her head playing sad ass love songs. If this wasn't a cry for help, I don't know what was. She didn't move an inch, even after I turned off the music. The only option that I had left was to jump on the bed and wake her up.

"Ahhh!" she screamed out. She focused her wide, bloodshot red eyes on me and then they turned into slits. "Really Kay, what the fuck is wrong with you? How long have your ass been here, and why the hell are you jumping on my damn bed?"

"Slow down, lil mama. I've been here for over an hour cleaning your nasty ass apartment. You should be ashamed of yourself. Wallowing in self-pity over a man that fucked you over." She went to open her mouth, but I had to stop it. "Aye, don't you even dare. My situation was different. Nonetheless, you are an amazing woman, and it's time you get off of your ass and enjoy this thing called life."

I grabbed her phone and flipped through Google Play. I found the perfect song, and we were going to dance this foolishness away. We were gonna get up and have a damn near perfect day if my life depended on it. I pressed play and smiled at her. In return, she rolled her eyes.

"Dearly beloved, we are gathered today to get through this thing

called life." Prince's song "Let's Go Crazy" began blasting through the sound system and Oya couldn't do anything but smile and shake her head. The song continued to play, and I began dancing around her room. She sat on that bed with her arms folded, and we couldn't have that. We were going to shake this shit off and have a good day.

After a few good tugs, she got her ass up and danced with me. The song played about four more times before I was good and tired. We ended up falling on the bed laughing. My plan worked, and Oya was now in better spirits.

"Okay, phase one complete. Get that ass up. We have things to do today." Surprisingly, she got up and got ready without me having to hold a knife to her throat. Today was going to be a good day.

The day went better than I expected. Brunch went off without a hitch, and we got some shopping done. We were able to take her mind off of everything that she's been going through. It felt good to have a bit of normalcy in our lives. Things haven't been easy by far, but I hope that this was the end of the storm for us.

Currently, we were getting ready to turn the night up a little bit. There was a huge party going on at one of our favorite clubs, and I felt that this was good for us. We needed one night to let loose, and we could worry about our troubles tomorrow.

We arrived at Club 312, and the line was wrapped around the corner. Thankfully, Oya did the owner's hair, so I was able to secure us a private section. When we stepped inside, the atmosphere was exactly what we needed. The DJ was going crazy, and immediately we grabbed drinks and started dancing. Tonight was gonna be a good night.

We were halfway through our night and halfway through our first bottle of liquor. Both of us were feeling better than we expected. Nothing was going to bring down the high that we were on, or so I thought. I was dancing and in a nice little groove when I felt a strong pair of hands around my waist, and I froze in place. I prayed for dear life that it wasn't Lorenzo, I can't deal with that tonight.

"Relax, you know I'm not gonna hurt you," Manahil's voice vibrated against my body and had me relaxed.

The DJ started playing The Bonfyre's song "Automatic", and we swayed back and forth. Then lights dimmed in the club and a spotlight shined at the entrance. The DJ started to announce who's birthday it was.

"Let's give it up for the man of the night. Happy Birthday, Zo! Ladies show him some love."

Lorenzo Lamont stumbled into the club with a bottle of Hennessy in his hand and a new chick on his arm. Thankfully, our section was towards the top of the club so we wouldn't be seen. Oya looked at me, and I let her know that I was good to go. I was so caught up in dancing with Manahil that I didn't even notice that Nix had joined us. Oya was now all smiles, and I'm positive that it came from him. Only time would tell if he was the right man for her.

"He's a good guy, Kay. She's in good hands," Hil whispered in my ear. "Stop worrying about them and let's focus on you. How are you feeling?"

"I'm good. I just want to enjoy the rest of my night with my people," I said as I brought his face to mine and placed small kisses on it.

I could feel someone staring a hole in the side of my face, and when I looked around, our eyes finally connected. Lorenzo was steaming hot mad, sitting in his section, taking a bottle of liquor to the head. He didn't scare me as much anymore, so I winked at him and wrapped my hands around Manahil's neck. My actions were petty and childish, but I wasn't going to let him have power over me any longer, enough was enough.

The four of us continued to enjoy our night and partied away. Lorenzo was a distant memory. We had a great time, but it was time to leave. Before we departed for the night, Oya and I went to the bathroom. She waited outside for me until I was finished. I was washing my hands, and a woman came and stood next to me and leaned against the wall.

"So you're the infamous Karma White. You're not as pretty as he made you sound," she spoke with slurred speech.

"And your name must be Insecurity if you're standing here judging my looks. Is there something that I can help you with?"

"Nah, I just wanted you to look me in my face and know that I'm the woman who took your man."

"Thank you for taking him. I wish both of you the absolute best. Make sure you know how to duck," I fired back.

She was pissing me off, and I needed her to get out of my face. I dried my hands and went past her toward the door but, she grabbed my arm and yanked me towards her.

"Don't walk away from me," she spoke through gritted teeth.

"Unless you want to become attached to that damn sink, you'll unhand me and go about your business." I pushed her off of me and left out before I did something I would regret.

"Everything okay?" Oya asked with a raised eyebrow. "I was about to come in there."

"Nah, everything is good," I said with a smile.

We grabbed hands and made our way out the front door where Hil and Nix were waiting. Oya and I valeted my car, so Hil and Nix chose to wait with us. I stood at his side and snaked my hand around his waist, and he kissed my forehead. Our little public displays of affection were making my heart flutter. Maybe he was the man that was made for me.

"Kay!"

The voice that I didn't want to hear was calling out my name from behind us. I wasn't going to deal with this shit, so I grabbed Hil's hand, and we started walking towards the end of the block. I would flag valet down when they pulled up.

"Kay, I know you hear me!"

Again, I ignored him, and I could feel the heat radiating off of Manahil's body.

"Ignore it. Please don't react."

No sooner than the words left my mouth, shots rang out behind us. Manahil pushed me, and I fell to the ground. He took off running as I screamed out. I had no clue where anyone was, and there was nothing I could do about it.

"Karma! Karma, where are you?" Oya yelled out as the shooting continued.

"Over here Ya. I'm over here!" She found me, and we ducked down behind a car. "Where is Nix? Did you see Manahil? He pushed me down and then took off running. Why would he do that? Oya, please let him be okay!"

"I don't know! He told me to run to the corner and find you. Oh God, I pray that they're okay," she cried as we hugged onto each other.

Police sirens wailed in the distance, and the shooting had stopped. When we thought the coast was clear, we took off running in search of Hil and Nix.

"Manahil! Where are you?"

There was chaos everywhere. People were trying to get to their cars and leave before anything else jumped off. One the ground by the entrance laid a man that had on similar clothes as Manahil. My mind wouldn't let me believe it was him until I walked up and saw Nix kneeling over him with a shirt covered in blood.

"Come on, bro. Stay with me. You gotta stay with me. Someone call a fuckin' ambulance!"

No, no, no, no, this could not be happening to me. I fell on my knees next to him and caressed his head. He cannot die on me. We were just figuring out what we were. Our future together was going to be bright together. As I held his head in my hands, I looked towards the street and saw Lorenzo standing there holding a bottle of liquor in one hand and a gun in the other. He was responsible, and no one could tell me otherwise.

"YOU DID THIS! YOU KILLED HIM! I swear on everything that I love I'm going to make you pay for this shit! You'll dream about me coming to your house and killing you with my bare hands. You and that bitch are going to see me, and I promise that Karma is going to come and collect! A life for a life. You better run while you can."

Fear danced in his eyes as he took off into the night.

"Hold on for me baby. Please hold on for me," I cried as Manahil drew his last few breaths. "Noooooooooooo!"

Made in the USA
Columbia, SC
06 September 2019